STAGECOACH
JUSTICE

ONE STAGECOACH, ONE SHOTGUN AND TWO HUNDRED POUNDS OF BAD ATTITUDE

THE ADVENTURES OF "STAGECOACH" MARY FIELDS, PIONEER FOR WOMEN'S RIGHTS IN THE MONTANA TERRITORY

A NOVEL BY

JAMES CICCONE

Stagecoach Justice
Copyright © 2021 by James Ciccone
Cover Design Livia Reasoner
Sundown Press
www.sundownpress.com

For Cynthia, Vincenzo, and Chloe Ciccone
This is the first book I've dedicated to them, but really,
everything I write is for them.

Also, for my sister, Diane Ciccone
I dedicated a poem to her in my teenage years, but I am
afraid that poem has been lost forever.

History, despite its wrenching pain, cannot be unlived, but if faced with courage, need not be lived again.

MAYA ANGELOU

Chapter One

Montana Territory, November 1885

The whole idea of justice got going good in my head the instant I hopped out of the passenger compartment of a finely upholstered Concord overland stagecoach with 10-gauge shotgun in hand.

Thinking back, Cascade, Montana wasn't exactly the kind of town where the idea of justice was likely to take root. It was a rancher's town cut out of blue mountains at an elevation that flirted with the clouds. Other than that, there wasn't much to it. There was really only sky, dust, wind, and the stagecoach.

The rest of what passed as the town was a cluster of clapboard shacks with mud roofs, a rickety boardwalk, two gas lamps, and a handful of hitching posts along the town's dusky main street. The cluster looked like a blemish on a prairie that was otherwise made perfectly majestic by a sky that was high and deep and all around.

We were a good two-day ride by stagecoach away from Helena. In other words, we were off in the middle of nowhere, a place so unfit for human habitation even the Crow elders had the good sense to reject it long ago to follow herds of buffaloes that roamed the prairie. The wind seemed to know of the place's shortcomings, too.

The wind disrespected Cascade whenever it pleased as it ran straight through clear to the other end of town and off to the prairie again without bothering to stop. And when the wind became jealous, it was free to grab at everything, the bunting attached to the buildings that lined the street, the un-furled curtains dancing in open windows, the red bandana around my neck, the apron over my dress, everything.

At the time, folks in this part of the Territories were quite unaccustomed to seeing the likes of me. The truth is, few places were. The country as a whole was isolated back then. The railroad hadn't even made its way out here yet.

Isolated or not, the sudden arrival of a negro woman stand-ing six feet tall and weighing two hundred pounds, a woman with the conspicuously oversized frame of a man, a very black woman puffing a black homemade cigar, wielding a shotgun, and brandishing a nasty disposition, the absolute spectacle of it, probably had a way of sending a chill, a sense of stunned curiosity really, through the bones of even the toughest ranch-ers, cattlemen, and farmers in these parts.

I was the first stranger to show up in these parts in years— and a colored woman, at that. I suppose that is the reason I inherited so many nicknames along the way, Stagecoach Mary, Black Mary, Nigger Mary, White Crow, and practically anything else folks set their minds on.

"I knew they was bound to have a saloon somewhere in this poor excuse for a town." I snapped, not bothering to look at the fellow still up on the coach's box. There was luggage to unload.

The six horses in the team dumbly raised and lowered their heads, waiting for the next command. Each time they moved, even slightly, the brass rings and chains on their leather har-nesses began to sing.

I hoisted my dress and apron above the knee and stomped off toward the saloon. I aimed to diffuse the notion that I was the type of retiring soul who would accept racial insult or any other form of disrespect from the folks of this town well before the idea got going in anyone's head.

Even in a rowdy place like a saloon, the sight of a shotgun had a way of convincing even the most recalcitrant soul that caution and decorum, if not outright respect, were mandatory at all times. Could I have handled things differently? Yes, I suppose, but, as a colored woman, or really anyone, if you didn't have the facility on your own to convince folks on the prairie they needed to respect your rights, there wasn't likely to be a lawman, politician, preacher, or anyone else for that matter who was likely to do it for you.

So, using every inch of my six-foot frame, I punched open the doors of the Silver Dollar saloon, tossed my shotgun against the wall, and surveyed the room.

It was a tough-looking and tough-smelling room. The men who crowded at the bar wore chaps, boots, spurs, and sombreros, and looked and smelled like they hadn't bothered in months to take a break from driving cattle, farming, or mining copper long enough to re-acquaint themselves with a straight razor, a bucket of warm water, and a bar of soap. There was a map of the Territories hanging in a frame on the wall behind the bar. Light from gas lamps danced everywhere. There was sawdust on the floor.

I picked out the toughest-looking rancher at the bar, a tall, wiry sort typical of the Montana Territory of the time, a no-nonsense individual wearing a leather vest and chaps who had been made tough and lean and confident by the rigors of long cattle drives, cruel winters, and disappointing springs, a man whose confidence showed in the way he leaned into the bar with most of his weight shifted casually to one hip.

I stood at the center of the saloon, hulking frame and all, a bona fide Republican, wearing a fancy dress.

Squinting with one eye, I lined up the rancher. The gentleman had no idea what was about to hit him.

"Shit," the rancher mumbled, looking away from the bar.

It was already too late.

Instead of simply sticking out my hand and offering to make his acquaintance, I launched a left-hand lead to the right side of his head. The punch exploded against his jaw. It spun his face away from the bar. He dropped to the floor. He was out cold.

The fight was over before it ever had a chance to begin. The punch that did the trick was a roundhouse hook, not a polite jab. It was the clean, measured, powerful, professional blow of a prize fighter, not the wild and wide swing of an amateur.

The punch triggered chaos in the crowd, even outrage. But not a single one of the men in the saloon, outrage aside, dared to intervene. Instead of taking me on, all six feet of me, the men exercised sound judgment, dismissed the incident, and attended to their fallen comrade. That was the safer course.

The rancher's limp body was prodded and consoled. The crowd urged him to get up, come to, do anything. His pride was at stake. But there would be neither pride nor revenge that day. Instead, there was only the rancher's deep moan. And with this single achievement, I had announced my arrival to Montana Territory.

Looking back, the thing I can tell you about rights is they are not real unless they are respected. There must be a constant demand for respect, and that demand must be taken seriously. If not, rights can be made to vanish. However, with the promise of a brawl or gunplay hanging in the balance, folks came to realize it was far easier to respect me than to suffer the consequences. By the time I punched the rancher, I was already good at showing folks the consequences.

I could brawl, smoke, curse, drink whiskey, hitch a team of horses, fend off wolves, bandits and robbers, shoot a shotgun, draw a pistol, tend to the sick and needy, and do a whole host of other things better than any man, white or colored. Why should anyone be allowed to pretend otherwise? The rancher was only the latest man to see things my way. The nasty disposition had everything to do with the trouble I had come through in life.

I respected Mr. Lincoln, and I had a habit of cursing and insisting on equal treatment for women in public. I wondered if any of the ranchers in Cascade were Republicans and felt the same way. I doubted it. They were probably Copperheads. Either way, I was sure they would have no problem respecting a punch in the nose.

By the age of thirty-two, I was no longer regarded as mere inventory on a slave master's ledger in Hickman County, Tennessee. Mr. Lincoln had seen to that. Having been born into slavery at or near 1832, 1833 or 1834, there was no clear record of my birth other than a journal entry listing me as estate property. So, I could not have said that bad luck began for me at birth, because I had no idea when I was born. And there were no records to help me figure it out either, no photographs, no certificates, no writings of any kind, nothing. My suspicion, though, was that bad luck had begun for me on the day I was born into slavery.

I had no experience with any other institution or lifestyle other than the one that had given me bad luck from the start, but I was determined to try to change. Thanks to Mr. Lincoln, I was finally free, free and flat broke.

I refused to go backward in life after the Emancipation. I was definitely not the type to linger on a plantation as a sharecropper. I needed to make my way out of the cruel institution on my own. So, I struggled to reach the glory and promise of the North and the household of Sister Mary Amadeus in Toledo, Ohio. There, I found work as a servant at the Ursuline Convent.

Sister Mary Amadeus's brother, Judge Dunne, had five children to raise alone following his wife Kate's untimely, and unfortunate, demise. So, Sister Amadeus and I took over. Judge Dunne, who made a fortune in the Philadelphia money market, had the foresight to hire help. I was the help he was looking for.

My relationship with Sister Amadeus, a relationship that actually started back on the plantation, quickly blossomed beyond the boundaries of the traditional master-slave relationship: We became fast friends. I gladly worked by her side for nearly five years, until Bishop Gilmore of Ohio called her to join Bishop Brondel of Helena to open a school to educate Blackfoot girls in the wilds of the Montana Territory. That's when everything changed.

The school was called St. Peter's Catholic Mission. While hunkering down in three cabins with mud roofs, and braving the cruel Montana winters, Sister Amadeus, a frail asthmatic, fell deathly ill with pneumonia. That's why I was dispatched to her side to work a miracle and nurse her back to health. That's also why I knew I had to insist on respect the instant I arrived in Cascade.

If it could be said the nation as a whole hadn't yet fully accepted the ideal of equality for a colored woman, or really any woman, and the federal government was obviously unprepared to do anything about it, the folks in Cascade weren't likely to do any better. Actually, they were likely to do far worse. However, this part of the Territories would quickly learn that I would not accept far worse or anything short of equality, and that I was both colored and a woman would not get in the way of it. My resolve, salty disposition, and fiery tongue would soon grow into legend.

In 1895, stories about me started hitting newspapers from as far away as the *Oregonian* in Portland, Oregon and as close as the *Weekly Gazette* in Billings, Montana. Of course, the reporters didn't get the stories straight or put real facts out there. Instead, they mentioned that I had a foul mouth, looked like a man, dressed like a man, drank whiskey like a man, and cursed like a man, stuff like that. However, none of that was exactly true. It was far worse. The truth was, I was a young woman who had survived the scourge of slavery, and my 'crass behavior', as they put it, and taste for stiff whiskey and a fight, were just getting started.

If there was any doubt about the truth of the stories about the things 'crass behavior' could achieve, my comically enlarged hands that had once been perfect for slavery, the .38 concealed beneath my apron, and my ability to fight like a man would provide more than sufficient corroboration.

The challenge I issued to the rancher and all comers in the saloon that day was my way of proving I was more than enough woman to do whatever I pleased in Montana, which included drinking whiskey at that saloon, despite the prohibition against women other than soiled doves setting foot in a saloon, moving wherever and whenever I pleased, and doing and saying whatever crossed my mind, and the whole of Montana would just have to learn to like it, regardless of local laws prohibiting women from doing any of the things on the long list of items I planned to do. And I planned to do plenty. Sure, complaints about my behavior began to bombard Bishop Brondel in Helena and ultimately threatened my welcome at the Mission, but that is getting way ahead of the story.

Chapter Two

When it came to avoiding a good fight or a stiff drink, I was probably not good at either. Actually, I was among the worse people at it in the entire Pacific Northwest. Take my first night in Cascade as an example. It was precisely the sort of thing that ultimately got me into trouble with the Catholic bishop in charge of the Mission. Instead of simply going straight to the Mission and minding my own business, I packed away my fancy dress, threw on a pair of men's trousers, and returned to the saloon.

I didn't care that there were bound to be more than a few fellows there who were still a little sore at me for knocking out the rancher earlier in the day.

The saloon was even rowdier at night than it was during the day. It seemed like it was pay day or something. There were bursts of laughter over the din of conversation. The sound of the solid glass bottoms of whiskey shot glasses hitting the bar cracked like gunfire. There was a fancy negro smiling and playing jumpy tunes on a standup piano.

There were card games going and smoking and cursing. Like the saloon in Miles City, the Silver Dollar doubled as a bawdy house, so there was a half-dozen or so fancy ladies working the room who wore lace dresses without backs, plunging necklines that showed more cleavage than the law allowed, and costume jewelry that sparkled. The men, on the other hand, smelled like chewing tobacco, the sweet smell of whiskey, and the stale air of livery stables. There was also the smell of armpits and crotches.

Outside, the night air from the prairie was crisp and clean. The ranchers had looped the reins of their horses over the wooden hitching rails in front of the saloon. The horses were busy at the water troughs, lifting their heads dumbly when the saloon racket became tumultuous. Teams of horses pulled wagons along the dusky street, moving in and out of shadows left everywhere by gas lanterns.

"You looking at me funny?" I asked one of the ranchers at the bar. His sardonic smile exposed missing teeth and a cocky attitude. I didn't like either.

"What? I got eyes, and the right to use them," the rancher said, stepping away from the bar. "You got a problem with that?"

"You heard me. Are *you* looking at *me* funny?" I spread my feet apart to hold my ground. I was at the center of the room approximately five paces away from the bar where the rancher stood.

"Suppose so."

"Suppose so?" I threatened, as the music stopped playing.

"Yeah, suppose *so*. I also reckon I *suppose* the likes of you ain't even supposed to be in no *saloon* in the first place, supposing that's what you actually is, is a woman. But by the looks of things, probably nobody is exactly sure what you is, except possibly you."

There was a blast of laughter.

"Oh, would you like to find out exactly what it is that I is and exactly what it is that I ain't?"

"Well, I got eyeballs to see exactly what *you is*," the rancher said, careful to emphasize the mangled grammar.

"Nah, you can't see what I is or you wouldn't dare say nothing like that at all. For example, you apparently can't tell that I ain't in no good spirits, can you? I just come off staging and ain't had a proper shot of whiskey in days. I had to jump out of that fine, red Concord coach I *paid* to ride in, scatter with the rest of the passengers, take cover, and open fire on bandits in order to run them off, and then open fire on the Sioux to run them off, too, just to get out here, and that was only the second day of the stage run.

"We had to push the coach out of the ruts you got everywhere in this Godforsaken excuse of a place called Montana more times than I could count. There were packs of Sioux and packs of wolves along the way seems like every damned mile. We lost exactly one wheel and one horse. The cliffs out here are so high it makes you dizzy to look down over the edge. When you do, you see silver clouds instead of brown earth.

"I had to listen to the passengers talk politics for over twenty days, and I did over thirty-two years of slavery before Mr. Lincoln had the good sense to sign the Emancipation, and to tell you the truth, I am not sure which was worse, thirty-two years of slavery or twenty days of listening to politics on a coach. If I had a choice, maybe I'd pick slavery."

"Slavery can be arranged again for you, if you like," cracked one of the ranchers at the far end of the bar.

This ignited still another burst of laughter.

"So whatever Mr. Lincoln said about the situation don't count out here for nothing, is that what you're telling me? So, what counts for out here, partner?"

"Slavery, stagecoach rides, your Mr. Lincoln, who also happens to be dead, or whatever else you got on your mind may or may not count, depending on who does the counting, but you still ain't allowed in no saloon in Montana, lady. That's what counts out here," the bartender interjected, looking up from the white cloth he was using to rub the bar. "That's the law out here, lady. No women allowed in the saloon by law, unless you happen to be a working lady. And by the looks of things, you ain't fit to be no working lady, not the type of saloon work we got out here for *ladies* anyway, if you get what I mean."

Those were fighting words. I turned away from the bartender. I raised my voice to address the entire saloon.

"Okay, I see what this is. Now, listen up. You got the nerve to have laws even in a place like this," I said in a loud and clear voice. "Tell you what I'm going to do. You got your laws alright, *men only* laws. I'll bet any man in here five bucks and a shot of whisky I can knock him out with just one punch. One punch! Any takers?"

A roar went up. The prospect of a contest could always be counted on to capture the imagination.

The bartender resumed rubbing the bar. The men laughed and prodded and gossiped and planned and pointed. The fancy ladies urged men to take the bet.

Suddenly, the rancher I insulted stepped away from the bar. "You got to show the money first, lady. I ain't fighting no lady for nothing. I need a stakeholder."

"Lady? I guess I just got a promotion! Look at that! Thank you, sir. Now, as for the rest of it. You don't need no stakeholder to be first," I said. "You need heart though. You first?"

He tried to trick me. He walked sideways like he was refusing the bet. Suddenly, he wheeled and threw up his hands.

Then, he walked straight into an uppercut. The punch moved his nose ever so slightly in the wrong direction. There was a lot of blood.

He grabbed at his nose, stumbled backward, and blended

into the crowd at the bar, beaten. The men at the bar roared mockingly at the sight of a woman punching a man.

"Bartender, that's one shot of whiskey on him, okay? Alright, who is next?" I demanded. I took the roar as a sign of disrespect, so I persisted. "Who is next? Let's go!"

At first, nobody was next.

Then, the next man mustered at least a little courage. He came forward, meekly. There was an audience. I didn't think he was much of a man. I was at least a head taller and several inches broader across the shoulders than this next man up.

"You boys remind me of those poor excuses for horses on the team that pulled my fancy red coach out here. They looked like rats, not horses, like y'all are closer to rats than men. I'll bet you miserable bastards didn't know that," I barely got the insult out before the rancher charged.

He put his head down as he ran. The brim of his Stetson made it impossible for him to see where he was going. It was cocked comically over his eyebrows. I couldn't see his eyes through the hat, and he couldn't see mine.

This didn't stop the charge. He was running at full gallop. Fortunately, I timed the run.

I spun. He missed. Instead of tackling me, he slid across the floor. The audience roared derisively.

"Get up, you silly sonofabitch!" a rancher shouted above the laughter.

Humiliated, the fallen rancher gathered his wits, rose, cursed, tossed off his Stetson, and charged yet again. I turned deftly, like a matador turns to escape the charge of a bull, and then I floored him with a check hook. There was no laughter. There were gasps. Then, there was silence.

"Bartender, make that two shots of whiskey and ten bucks. Seems like there is plenty of work in this saloon after all, ain't there? And it pays quite well, too."

It was customary for patrons to disarm themselves upon entering a saloon in the territories. They voluntarily complied with the custom and leaned their shotguns against the walls inside the saloon before proceeding to the bar to commence acting like fools. So, I didn't fear gunplay. Besides, although I gave up my shotgun at the door, I still had my .38 strapped to my leg. Like always, it was concealed.

This time, two men charged at once. I didn't think that made for a fair fight. It didn't matter what I thought. It was going to be a fight anyway, a two on one affair.

There were no fair fights anywhere in the Pacific Northwest, for there were no rules. There were only fights. Nevertheless, I wasn't tempted to draw the .38. The threat really wasn't that serious.

This wasn't the first time I fought two men at the same time either, and it probably would not be the last time. Timing and patience were everything against those odds. I waited. I figured the two of them would swing wildly. They didn't disappoint.

They made the mistake of alternating runs. The men didn't give me the respect of attacking at the same time. That would have presented a greater danger. That was an error in calculation.

The first one swung so wildly he toppled himself to the floor. This ignited a blast of laughter. There was gossiping and finger pointing among the ladies. Of course, I didn't care, and I didn't give the fellow the luxury of allowing him to climb to his feet. I knocked him out cold right then and there.

He spilled over backward. That was the end of the first one. "Hell, don't you boys practice fighting out here?" I taunted. There wasn't time for repartee. The second of the pair was on his way. He, too, caught only air with his wild swing. However, he didn't end up on the floor. He kept his balance. He bounced around on his toes. He wanted more.

He threw several combinations. None of them landed. I could tell this one had some training as a boxer, probably a man transplanted out here from one of the big cities of the North. He was slick.

He wasn't likely to fold after one blow, and the bet was that I could knock him out with one punch. Sensing someone might raise a technicality and deprive me of my five bucks if I didn't knock him out with a single clean shot, I waited. I didn't swing. I ducked, bobbed, circled, and moved instead, careful to stay out of range.

He made the mistake of stepping inside my wingspan. I hammered him. The punch sent him to floor. Like the others, once on the floor, he showed no courage. The contest was over. And with this incident, I had earned my first pay day in Montana, twenty bucks and four shots of whiskey.

The music played again. The ladies laughed and worked the room. The card games and conversations resumed. I made my way to the bar to collect the debt.

"Lady, you can collect your winnings now, fair is fair," the bartender said. "However, the law is the law, and you are not allowed inside the saloon, ever. There is an ordinance against it."

"Ain't that surprising! The law made it all the way out here to a place like this and bothered to stop! Well, you, sir, you can tell the law that I aim to drink wherever and whenever I like, and by the way, whenever I like is generally every day, and wherever I like is right here. Where's my money?"

The bartender served the whiskey, four shot glasses at the same time. He slid the twenty bucks, Union currency, across the bar, "I was only being a gentleman to tell you the rules, lady. I don't know where you're from, but this is Montana. Things are different here."

"I can see that. Y'all can't fight a lick here. How do you survive against the Indians?" I threw back the shots one by one.

"Guns," he said.

"Good answer," I laughed.

"That was one fancy red coach you rode into town with, lady. How did you get the chance to ride one of them? Did you rob it?"

"I paid the fare is how. I rode into Miles City on the Pacific Northern, and I sat on an upholstered seat, too."

"Paid the fare."

"Yup, ain't that how you ride one of them trains, pay the fare?"

"And another thing, I may not know exactly what you paid to get out here, but I do know exactly what you are," the bartender declared.

"What might that be?"

"You are a nigger."

"A what?"

"You heard me right, a nigger."

"You got no right to talk to me like that."

"I do."

"You do?"

"It is called the First Amendment of the U.S. Constitution, the freedom of speech."

"You got the freedom of speech to call me a nigger?"

"Yup."

"If the Constitution ain't rigged, the Supreme Court must be, if that's what it says. That word ain't no part of speech. That's part of fighting words. It ain't nothing to protect, let alone something for our beautiful Constitution to protect. It is beneath the dignity of the land out here. It is beneath the dignity of the Constitution. It is pure hate speech. It shouldn't take a judge to figure that out. I know a whole lot more about them judges in Washington than you think.

"First up, they ain't called judges. They're called *justices*.

"Second up, hate speech ain't even speech at all. Hate speech is like a punch when there ain't no agreement to fight, like a crime. It don't qualify as speech under the Constitution, unless you rig the Constitution, so the Constitution shouldn't even apply. You got the right to carry a gun, but you ain't got no right to murder nobody with it. You got the right to speak, but you ain't got no right to call nobody a nigger.

"Now, turn that around backwards. If the Constitution gave you freedom of speech, and that freedom gave you the right to call out somebody as a nigger and use that freedom to say whatever you see fit—including using a word that stings like nigger—and you extended that logic to the right to carry a gun, the right to carry a gun would also give you the right to use it any way you see fit, including murder. That's backward logic, and it's absurd.

"You don't have to go to school a day to figure it out, either. The country cannot heal the open wounds of the Civil War when the Supreme Court signals that hate is still alive and well. The word is a thing of hate. The Constitution is a thing of beauty. The Constitution shouldn't be made to protect ugly, --and a word like *nigger* is one ugly word—or any of the other ugly words on the list of ugly words, any more than it should be made to protect a punch, or a gunshot, or a rape. Those are crimes, and calling me a nigger is a crime.

"Now, call me nigger again, *boy*, and you'll get what them ranchers on the floor over there got and worse, hear?"

I took my time lighting a black homemade cigar. I blew the smoke anywhere I pleased. The smell of cigar smoke was sweet. It covered the smell of armpits and crotches.

"Nobody buys that idea. You were just a slave, said so yourself. The Supreme Court ain't used to the idea of protecting the likes of you." The bartender seemed unwilling to give up the point.

"Maybe somebody will do something with the idea sooner or later," I countered.

"I'd like to get sworn in to Congress one day, too, sooner or later; but the problem is, you have to win an election…and sooner or later never comes," the bartender said, watching the bar he was rubbing.

This ended the debate, but not the controversy. I knew the bartender was more correct than he realized. Judge Dunne served on that Court in Washington, and he owned slaves. I knew it. I was one of them.

Judicial temperament aside, Judge Dunne wasn't likely to cast a vote against his own interests. The freedom to use hate speech was at the root of the ideology that made slavery possible, chapter and verse. The things done to negroes across the land were not wounds. They were deep holes of hypocrisy threatening to swallow the whole society. Somehow, the local law prohibiting women from drinking whiskey in a saloon was strangely related. I knew you really couldn't trust the law, unless you wrote it yourself. That's exactly what I planned to do, rewrite the law.

Chapter Three

Mississippi River, June 1870

The paddle-wheels were silent, but the gangplank leading to the main deck of the magnificent steamboat was crowded with men loading luggage and supplies, passengers scurrying about, and smartly dressed officers, porters, and crew tending to their duties.

The steamboat, the Robert E. Lee, was parked at a levee preparing to launch on a trip up the Mississippi River from New Orleans to St. Louis. It was the summer of 1870—June 30th to be exact. I saw her standing there bobbing stately in the brown water. This was long before I paid Montana any mind.

I had no way of knowing at the time that by satisfying my urge to walk the gangplank of that magnificent boat, blend in with the workers, and stowaway, I would join the most famous steamboat race in American history, the race up the Mississippi from New Orleans to St. Louis between the Robert E. Lee and the Natchez VII. The Natchez owned the speed record having once completing the 1,278 miles in three days, twenty-one hours, and fifty-eight minutes.

The first thing I wanted to do after the Emancipation was flee the South, like a bad dream. I imagined the sheer power of that steamboat's paddle-wheels beating away at the brown face of the Mississippi River would carry me to the glory and promise of the North and closer to the ideal of freedom. This was at a time in my life before I knew anything about Sister Amadeus's plight to build the Mission for Blackfoot girls in the wilds of Montana. However, without the daring and courage it took to climb the gangplank of the Robert E. Lee, our lives probably would not have intersected later at the Mission.

Nerves tore at my guts as I walked the gangplank. I didn't have the money for the fare. I didn't even have the money to buy a newspaper.

My only chance was to stow away, tricky as that sounded, given the criminal penalties imposed for the arrest of stowaways in Louisiana. I still remembered slavery, so the last thing I wanted to do was find my way into chains. I was too nervous to notice any outward sign the boat was preparing for a race through history that would guarantee the victor a place in immortality. It was crucial that I study the bustle around the loading process to spot an opening to get on the boat without detection.

The early morning summer sky over downtown New Orleans was still cloudless. The massive sidewheels of the boat were still silent. The Mississippi was silent, too.

The Robert E. Lee symbolized speed, power, and progress. She was 285 and 1/2 feet long from stern to bow, forty-six feet across on her main deck, cost nearly a quarter of a million dollars to build, and sparkled in the sun. The very name Robert E. Lee painted in elegant block letters on the wheel-houses announced class, confidence, and prestige. To me, she symbolized hope.

If I could just successfully climb her gangplank and stowaway, the Robert E. Lee would offer a way out of my troubles in the South. In the North, I expected to find the glory and freedom that Mr. Lincoln promised.

Simply put, the "Monarch of the Mississippi," as she was

called, was an indomitable boat on an indomitable river in an indomitable nation during an indomitable era. She was touted as the most powerful and luxurious steamboat of her generation. Built in New Albany, Indiana during the Civil War, her accommodations were marked by splendor and excess.

There were sixty-one staterooms in her main cabin, a nursery, and twenty-four extra rooms in the Texas for passengers and officers. The elegant furniture in the main cabin was made of rosewood. There was a velvet carpet nearly eighteen feet wide and 225 feet long rolled over the main cabin's marble floor. The seat cushions on the chairs set around the boat's twenty dining tables were made of crimson satin. There were skylights of stained glass, arched ceilings, dazzling chandeliers, rosewood doors, and fancy inlaid gold scrollwork everywhere. The palatial accommodations represented only a fraction of the boat's prowess. The engineering below the main deck was her real story. It was pure genius.

The shafts were made of iron, weighed nearly 20,000 pounds, and were each twenty-three feet long. The cranks alone weighed 6,000 pounds. Above the deck, a complex system of rigging and canvas sheaves announced the boat's superiority to all who saw her. Her stacks, mast, and sidewheels were gigantic. Below the deck, she reportedly possessed the largest twin high-pressure steam engines on the Mississippi.

The engines were built for audacious displays of speed and power. They were designed to push the sidewheels to speeds that tested the laws of physics. The eight boilers that fed massive volumes of water to the engines were absolute infernos with insatiable appetites for coal and other fuel. In case of fire, explosion, or other mishap, three pumping fire engines and hoses stood at the ready. In every respect, this boat was a flawless gem, a testament to American ingenuity. But, was she faster than her rival boat, the Natchez? That was the question.

There was action everywhere on the main deck. There were boys wearing floppy newsboy hats who hawked week old newspapers for six cents a copy, men with bushy Civil War-era goatees, wing beards and burnsides wearing navy blue and black tailored three piece suits with wide lapels, women who wore bright colored satin dresses layered like wedding cakes and elaborate broad brimmed hats adorned with flowers and netting atop their heads, and the crew scurrying about, unpacking luggage and supplies at horse-drawn coaches, hauling the cargo onboard, and attending to other small matters of the boat's invited guests. In the commotion, I managed to slip on board.

I spotted a colored man huddled with a group of Creole girls. He was fat and laughed a lot. Sometimes, he threw back his head and laughed with his mouth wide open, exposing his entire dental plate which included a gold tooth. When he wasn't laughing, he was peppering the girls with questions about what was expected of them as chamber maids.

I wanted to find work on the boat, too, but I seriously doubted that at my height and weight I was cut out for the work of a chamber maid. The Creole girls, on the other hand, were absolutely perfect. They were stunningly beautiful. Few, if any, women could compete with their caramel skin, flowing tresses, and perfect waistlines.

I decided not to bother to try to compete with them for the job of chambermaid. I figured it might get me kicked off the boat if I tried. Instead, I tried to steal past the gathering without detection.

"Y-y-you. Hey, you," the colored man said, stuttering. The words came out like he had two tongues, and one of them was used to getting in the way of the other.

I looked away and pretended not to hear.

"H-h-hey, y-y-you, I say!"

I kept walking.

"Come h-h-here r-r-r, right-t-t-t... now," he insisted.

I complied.

"Y-y-y-you looking f-f-for w-w-work, here?" he gasped.

"Y-y-yes," I said, mockingly.

The Creole girls laughed.

The sight of a six-foot tall woman weighing 200 pounds who slipped onto the boat without permission and possessed the audacity to mock the speech impediment of the one man on the boat who could save her hide from arrest and far worse was indeed comical. How does a 200-pound woman hide on a boat?

"Y-y-y-y-you have ex-ex-ex-experience as a chamber maid?"

"No, but I think I can catch on fast. Are you sure I am chamber maid material?"

"Not, not, not, not at all s-sure about you," he said, closing his eyes as he spoke. "But, but, but you got a strong back and can probably do more work on the boat than a man and for half the pay, so you're hired."

I didn't like the sound of "half the pay." It didn't matter. I had no options. The fat man showed me the dining room, the kitchen, the cabins, and the laundry. That's where I would spend the next three or four days. I felt so fortunate to find work on the boat. I was even given my own cabin.

Back on the main deck, I spotted a white man who looked as though he was in charge of the entire operation, not just the chamber maids. He was ordering crew members around. He was dressed in a black suit. He wore leather shoes without a single scuff mark. His white hair was slick and combed toward the back of his head. His bushy white goatee and burn-sides matched the hair on top of his head.

"Get up there, and take her all down," he demanded, point-ing skyward at the mast.

The crew member shimmied up the pole, unscrewed the mast in sections, and took it down. Other men worked at dis-assembling canvas sheaths and rods and whatever loose rig-ging they could get their hands on. Several crew members had scaled poles to bring down flags and banners that had once been proudly unfurled.

"Who is he?" I asked my boss.

"He's Captain J.W. Cannon." The boss didn't stutter for the first time. He pronounced the captain's name as though it was magical or even Biblical.

"But why are they taking down all of the rigging?" I asked, as a crowd began to form to watch the work.

"The captain is a master strategist, is why," one of the pas-sengers interjected, pointing at the mast. "He's taking down all of the rigging so there isn't any rigging to catch the wind and slow down the boat when we head up the Mississippi. He is stripping the boat clean of all unnecessary parts. He already limited the weight the boat is carrying to only a few invited guests, no excess baggage or supplies, and so on. This isn't an ordinary trip to St. Louis. It is a race against a rival boat, the Natchez, and the captain aims to not just beat the Natchez in this race, but also to break the speed record set by the Natchez back in June, too. The distance between New Orleans and St. Louis is 1,287 miles, and the Natchez did it in three days, twenty-one hours, and fifty-eight minutes back in June."

"Y-y-yup," said the boss of the chamber maids.

"The boats are comparable. Sure, we have powerful twin engines, and our boat is slightly over 285 feet long and their boat is slightly over 300 feet long. Both boats have the same number of boilers, eight. The Natchez has a reputation for owning a capacity to carry more weight, true, but at the end of the day the boats are of comparable capacity, what a match race, what a spectacle! I am betting the difference is strategy, brain power. Our boat is commanded by a tactical genius, Captain J.W. Cannon. The Natchez is commanded by Captain Leathers. Everybody around the civilized world knows about this race all the way to Europe. They got men stationed at intervals along the banks to report the time and progress of the race and cable the news to all parts of the States and Europe. And think of the money wagered. It has got to be one million bucks if it is a penny. The difference isn't the capacity of the boats. That is comparable. The difference is the capacity of the brains of the men who command the boats. That is the secret unknown to the betting public. That is where the real contest lies." The passenger lit a cigar. Cigar smoke began to fill the air.

I overcame the urge to ask the passenger for a drag off his cigar. I left for the kitchen. I began work with the other servants there.

I worked hard to help prepare the evening's massive dinner. Nevertheless, I felt the boat pull away from the levee. There were rumors that we set off five minutes ahead of the Natchez, so we were the lead boat. Some of the men in the kitchen felt this was poor strategy.

By pulling off on the lead, the Natchez could stalk our boat. From this vantage point, their captain could time the winning move. Plus, the Natchez wouldn't waste fuel if the headwinds were strong.

The problem with steamboats was they required constant raging fires in the boilers to convert water into pressurized steam in order to keep the side-wheels turning. The boats only carried a limited amount of coal below the deck. The boats were only designed to carry a limited amount of weight. That coal was literally devoured by the infernos in the boat's eight boilers. The boats needed to refuel with coal deliveries to the boat about every 100 miles or so at the banks of the river. These stops cost the boats precious time.

Later, one of the servants showed me the boilers below the deck. Men were stripped to the waste shoveling coal nonstop into the raging infernos. The flames inside the boilers were white and blue and yellow. They seemed to leap at the coal and yearn for more.

It was mercilessly hot there. Sweat poured off the men, but they didn't stop shoveling coal. They couldn't stop. If they stopped, the boat would stop, too.

That night, I retired to my cabin. I wasn't there five minutes before there was a knock on the door. It was the boss.

"H-h-hey, l-l-lady," he said, stammering as usual.

"Yes," I answered, purposely leaving open the cabin door.

"I-I-I w-w-want to s-s-s-see what you got under that pretty dress, lady." He had his eyes closed. He wouldn't have been able to see what was under my dress at that moment, even if I agreed to oblige and lift it.

"What!"

"You heard. Y-y-you think I give away j-j-j-jobs on the b-boat for f-f-f-f-free?"

The boss reached for the hem of my dress. I pushed him away.

"Here, boss. You want to see what's under this dress so bad, do you?"

I pulled the door closed to give him a closer look. I pushed him onto the bed. He smiled broadly and began unfastening his clothes. His gold tooth sparkled. I reached under my dress. Instead of bloomers, I pulled out the .38 and trained it on the boss's forehead.

Suddenly, the boss was no longer amorous. He didn't talk. He closed his mouth. The gold tooth that once flashed was now concealed. If he had two tongues, neither one was of service to him at this moment.

"Now, you fasten up your clothes," I said slowly, careful to hold the .38 steady. "And you…get. Otherwise, this pistol'll give you more of a good time than you can handle, a blast in fact."

He nervously tried to both fastened his clothes and escape at the same time. I held the cabin door shut with my toe.

"Hold it, and one more thing," I said. "That half pay you offered for me doing the same work as a man, you can double it now, and we have a deal. I don't think the captain would appreciate hearing what is going on in his boat. Let's just call double the pay payment in full for a secret. I like the sound of equal pay for equal work, don't you?" I heard the slogan somewhere before, but couldn't remember where. It didn't matter. I used it anyway.

The boss waved his hand dismissively and left. I strapped the pistol to my leg. I walked out into the open air on the main deck.

Our boat was pulling alongside a barge.

"What's going on?" I asked one of the crew members.

"We are getting coal off that barge to refuel," the crew member said. "Notice, we ain't stopping, and our engines still have steam. We are only slowing to refuel while the Natchez has come to a dead stop on the banks about ten minutes back. Their captain gets coal deliveries on the banks at designated stops along the river. This means they have to stop their boat.

Captain Cannon has an entire network of floating barges up the river to deliver coal to the Robert E. Lee on the fly. There will be no stopping for us. There will be little, if any, loss of time."

The boat ahead of the battling boats reported the shift in tactics by telegraph to the newspapers and indeed the entire civilized world. The Robert E. Lee was already in the lead by over ten minutes, and we had only recently met nightfall on the first day of the race.

I didn't realize it at the time, but after I fell asleep that night, the Robert E. Lee blew a steam pipe. This let the Natchez close in on us. She was within only a few minutes of us before we got the pipe repaired, got going again, and pulled away.

This was turning out to not only be a contest of sheer speed and power, but a contest that ultimately would depend on tactics and endurance. Victory doesn't always belong to the swiftest or the smartest or the most powerful. So, the question, as it turned out, wasn't who had the faster boat. The question was, which boat would arrive at the finish line first. The thousands of spectators along the banks of the Mississippi, and the many more fanatics witnessing the event over telegraph wire elsewhere, learned the very same lesson: Victory is a wise and unforgiving judge. She belongs only to the competitor who hits the finish line first.

As the race wore on, the pattern of meeting a barge every 100 miles for coal, while the Natchez stopped at the banks, began to cost the Natchez time. There were false reports that Captain Leathers had taken on a full load of cargo and passengers while Captain Cannon hadn't accepted his regular load, accepting only seventy-five invited guests, and this shift in the weights had become the deciding factor in the race. But the shift in the weights wasn't the real story.

The real story was that Captain Leathers had to stop his boat every 100 miles to get coal. This meant his boat's engines stopped, too. It took approximately ten minutes to rebuild steam in the engines. His strategy was to drop off cargo at each stop to lighten his load. It represented a serious miscalculation. He had underestimated the ingenuity of his adversary. Conversely, Captain Cannon made no such error in judgment. He saw the stops as opportunities to gain a tactical advantage.

On each bend of the sinuous Mississippi, in every place where there was human habitation, we saw hundreds, if not thousands, of people cheering the spectacle. On the second day, our boat passed Natchez, the town on the Mississippi that served as the namesake of our rival boat. I was doing the work of ten men in the kitchen, dining room, the nursery, or wherever I could pitch in to help the effort.

The Mississippi River bends sharply to the east and back again to the west at Vicksburg. At this point of the race, we were able to spot the smoke from the stacks of the Natchez off in the distance. Captain Cannon's strategy aside, there was only about one mile separating the boats at this juncture of the race.

Sensing the possibility of defeat, the captain ordered the men to work nonstop at the boilers. The steam didn't stop hissing. The engines didn't stop turning. The paddle-wheels didn't stop spinning. The work didn't stop. It couldn't.

This went on from dawn to dusk and back to dawn again without failure or delay. At Memphis, it looked as though our fortunes had changed, and the Robert E. Lee had a lock on victory. The reason is we had a system of barges ahead to refuel and plenty of time and distance already separating us from our rival, and the Natchez enjoyed no such advantage. The Natchez headed to the banks at various points of the race to get more coal. The idea to drop off cargo to lighten the load was not a stroke of genius. It was a failed strategy.

On the banks and wharfs at Memphis, there were thousands of people waving and cheering us on, and as we cleared Memphis, heavy fog began to descend over the Mississippi. It was visible in the distance from our stern, but the going ahead was crystal clear. This meant the Natchez was heading for the dangers of the fog, and we were just in the clear of it as we proceeded upriver.

The prospect of a low water level and thick fog meant Captain Leathers would cut his engines. He couldn't risk catastrophe and the lives of his passengers. Meanwhile, we didn't experience any such hazard. It was full speed ahead. The message wired over the cable was that the fog delay had cost the Natchez six hours. Thusly, we had achieved an insurmountable lead. Victory was within reach.

We went about our chores confidently. We believed the only contest was whether we would break the Natchez's record. The challenge of the Natchez was moot. We were already gloating. We were wrong.

We were wrong due to mathematical error. The last barge in the network was at a greater distance than 100 miles out of St. Louis. It wasn't Captain Cannon's error. It was the error of the barge's pilot. He was supposed to meet us north of Cape Girardeau. Instead, he met us south of that destination. That meant we could conceivably run out of fuel before we reached St. Louis. If our boat ran out of coal and stopped, we would lose, even if we were many hours ahead of the Natchez. Eventually, the Natchez would pass a stopped boat. The race, and the record, everything, would be lost.

This fate began to befall us north of Chester. The men at the boilers screamed. They were nearly out of coal. This would cause the engines to lose steam and fail. The paddle-wheels would cease turning. We would suffer the ignominy of surrendering a huge lead due to folly, a majestic boat, a powerful boat, dead in the water and bobbing helplessly.

The captain grew frantic. He pled with the fire men at the boilers to shovel coal even faster. They complied, until there was no coal left to shovel.

At the captain's command, the servants and crew began breaking up furniture. They hustled the wood below deck. The fires roared yet again. The twin engines hissed. The paddle-wheels thrashed at the water. We were moving.

We were north of Chester, only a stone's throw from St. Louis. However, tragedy visited us yet again. We were out of furniture. The fires were virtually out. The paddle-wheels no longer aggressively attacked the river. The boat listed to the left. The captain was out of ideas. I wasn't.

I went to the kitchen and wrapped up as much pork as I could get my hands on. I packed hundreds of pounds of ham butts and bacon strips with plenty of white, greasy fat, and I sent the kitchen help to the boilers with the bundles. The instant that pork grease was cast into the boilers through the open boiler doors, the flames leapt with approval, and the paddle-wheels began to grind once again. We were moving. A cheer went up!

I kept sending pork below the deck, and the paddle-wheels kept turning. We sped along the river in the sunshine to thousands of adoring fans as we pulled up to the docks in St. Louis. We arrived! We were victorious! We were a full six hours ahead of Captain Leather's boat!

The Natchez was still laboring. We had beaten the rival boat! Nevertheless, one issue remained. Had we set the speed record?

The people of St. Louis turned out in record numbers to watch us arrive. It was July 4, 1870, at approximately 6:00 p.m. The thousands of people on the docks reminded me of the crowds that gather to witness the spectacle of a thoroughbred horse race, a prize fight, or a hanging. The boat timing the event and sending telegraphs updating the events surrounding the contest by cable around the world clocked us in at three days, eighteen hours, and fourteen minutes. The mighty Robert E. Lee, armed with its amazing captain and capable crew, had indeed broken the record with the help of broken furniture and plenty of lard.

Chapter Four

Cascade, Montana, May 1913

While I was waiting in the news room of the *Cascade Courier*, I had a chance to look back on it all: the time I hopped out of the red Concord Overland stagecoach on my first day in Montana and went straight to the saloon, where I announced my arrival by delivering a knockout punch to the first rancher who looked at me sideways; the time I went to the saloon later that same day not to apologize, but to offer a bet of five bucks and a shot of whiskey to any man bold enough to take me on; and the time I stoked the boiler fires below the main deck of the Robert E. Lee with pork.

I was ready to explain to the reporter who was writing my life story that these things were only a small part of my life, only a small part of the reason the mayor of Cascade was preparing a ceremony to announce that I was a pioneer for women's rights—really, *human* rights—and why he was so sure my life was part of the legend of the Old West. I wanted to get it all off my chest to the reporter, like the interview was a confession of sorts. I was eighty-one years old. I guess you could say I was running out of time.

The year was 1913. The mayor of Cascade was planning to unveil a formal photograph of me that was on file at the Ursuline Convent offices. I was wearing a fancy dress with an adoring dog at my feet in the photograph. And, of course, I was holding a shotgun. It was a formal pose. However, it wasn't at all symbolic of what I had really gone through during my life in Montana.

The mayor was preparing to announce at the unveiling ceremony that the town would celebrate my birthday each year on March 15th, so folks could remember the old days of the Western frontier and how rapidly our society evolved. However, the truth was I didn't know my real birth day, so they couldn't possibly know what day to celebrate any more than I did, but I liked the idea.

Conversely, I didn't like the bigotry that was left over from slavery, and there were more than a few bigots in Montana. The bigots held sway for most of my life, except I had a temper and a way about me that was more than a match for bigotry.

Looking back, I learned how to master my surroundings, the wolves, the bitter winters, the blazing hot summers, the bandits, the horses, the stagecoach runs—and later, the Star Route runs to deliver mail for the U.S. Postal Service, the hard labor at the Mission—and, above all, the people who didn't believe a colored woman, or any woman for that matter, had any say in nothing.

I suppose being six feet tall, packing a .38, a shotgun, and a jug of whiskey, and sporting a bad temper didn't hurt matters any. Put it all together, I would say I was more than enough woman to earn my reputation as the terror of the countryside. However, I would say my absolute best quality, the quality that stood above all others, was my speed and accuracy with the .38 I packed beneath my apron. In Montana, without the .38 and the skill to use it, all of the other qualities meant absolutely nothing.

The locals boasted that I was a deadly shot anywhere inside of fifty paces, and that I could both snap the hind leg off a fly that lit upon a horse's ear with the business end of a whip and shoot the fly in the eye with a pistol at the same time. Rumors like that about me weren't exactly true. It was far worse.

The folks of Cascade hurt me into finding ways to make them accept me, and they ended up doing just that, accepting me. There was still something that wasn't quite right across the rest of the country. There was something missing. There was something about respecting the rights of others that hadn't quite evolved. I never fully grasped why it was taking so long for folks to respect what Mr. Lincoln started. They were hanging on to the past.

I never forgot slavery. How could I? But I let the bitterness go before I arrived in Montana. I wasn't sure why everyone else couldn't do the same, and if they couldn't let go, I also wondered why they weren't *made* to let go. It was simple. The men around Cascade figured out it wasn't a good idea to talk to me wrong whether they had let go of the idea or not. I'd take the cigar out of mouth, size them up, curse them out, and invite them to trade punches. And if punching didn't work, the .38 would do the trick. It was Montana. It was the 1800s. It was wild.

I heard the mayor was expecting a huge crowd—hundreds of people—to watch the ceremony to hang my portrait, like the ceremony was a prize fight, a presidential debate, a lynching, or a horse race. I reckoned they were coming from everywhere to watch the end of my story, the story of the notorious "Stagecoach" Mary Fields, pioneer.

The sound of the telegraph printing out the news over the wire in the *Cascade Courier's* newsroom cut through my daydream. I reckoned the reporter would be back soon. Then, I spotted the reporter. He ran hurriedly down the hallway wearing a black coat with wide lapels, a fine coat similar to the one Captain Cannon wore aboard the Robert E. Lee. The reporter seemed like he was under pressure to meet a deadline.

He had a chubby face, soft, clever hands, and clipped fingernails. The color beneath his fingernails was a fading pink, which was the same color as his face. His silver-rimmed spectacles left dents at the tops of his cheeks. The lenses were thick, and they magnified his eyes to sheer enormity.

He looked nervous, out of breath, as though he himself owned a life story that one day would be celebrated, and those huge eyes were unforgettable. His spectacles rose and fell on his nose with the tumult of his breathing. I was mesmerized by the way the lenses caught and reflected the light, almost like I could escape it all if only I had the will to stare at the shiny lenses long enough.

At first, he whispered. "Do you feel you were treated fairly here in Cascade back in the 1880s?" His chest was still heaving.

"No," I replied.

I wondered why he was still so nervous, so out of breath. If talking to an 81-year-old colored woman made him this nervous, he should have tried his luck at standing in my place as a slave in Hickman County, Tennessee, I thought.

"No?" the reporter hissed.

"How would you feel if you were once a slave and was asked a question like that? How would you feel if you were excluded from a saloon, a stagecoach, or anything else in your lifetime?"

"Not good, I suppose," he conceded. "Is there anything else you'd like to add about it?"

"Yes," I said. I spat at the floor.

"And what might that be?"

"I'd like to add a cigar and a shot of whiskey if you got any handy. That is my way of reminiscing. Hold the talk. Pour the whiskey."

The reporter laughed.

"By the way, I wasn't joking."

"Seriously, I heard even now, you are not welcome every-where in town—like the Ladies Aid, the auxiliaries, the socie-ties, and the guilds."

"Technically not true. You see, I never bothered to apply for membership, so you can't say I was excluded. But the rea-son I didn't apply is because I knew, like everybody knows, colored people are not welcome, so we need not apply. It is still a white town. For example, once they got to know you, they might do anything for you on the street, let you go to the saloon, let you deliver the mail and run supplies, babysit their children for $1.50 a day, even hang your picture up some-where, but they weren't likely to invite you to stay in their homes or even sit down at their table to eat a meal. Do you get the picture?"

"I see. You never got married or had children either, did you?"

"I hope you're not going to hold that one against me, are you?" I laughed.

"No, I'm just making a record."

"I was the only colored woman in Cascade, and I was big-ger and uglier than any man here, so who was I going to marry? In the beginning, I got called a wild beast because I drank whiskey, I swore, and I was a Republican—the political party of Mr. Lincoln. Well, I must have been a wild beast then, because I pled guilty to being all three."

"I heard you got fired by Bishop Brondel for dueling with the janitor out at the Mission, cursing, smoking cigars, fighting men, hanging out in the saloon, drinking whiskey? Is any of that true?"

"Where ever did you hear such a thing? Lies... No, actually, most of it *is* true, but I got fired alright, but not for the reasons you mentioned. Truth is, I shouldn't have been fired at all, and Sister Amadeus didn't want me to go. How was it fair for the bishop to fire me without a hearing? He didn't witness the incident. It was all hearsay. He didn't know what happened.

"I was denied my day in court. I told the bishop I wanted a hearing. He wouldn't give me one. I wanted him to see if there were any witnesses to testify that they saw me duel the janitor, because it didn't happen. That white man was jealous that a woman was getting more pay than he was. And I was getting more pay than he was because I was doing more work than he was, okay? Fair is fair.

"And I never had a duel. It never came to that. Sure, I drew my pistol. That's what you did in Montana in the 1890s. If you didn't draw, you wouldn't necessarily live to regret it. He was ready to draw on me. I was just quicker and drew first is all.

"Now, the rest of it was true, the part about the fighting, cussing, drinking, and carrying on, but that wasn't nothing new. It hadn't been a reason to fire me for the eight years I was there. I know for a fact the priests and bishops were up to far worse than fighting, cussing, drinking, and carrying on." I ended the point with a wink of my right eye.

I didn't plan to let the conversation end there, not that you'd necessarily consider the exchange much of a conversation. In my book, there was plenty more to explain than what the mayor and newspaper reporter talked about.

The mayor was a gracious man. He complimented me as one of only a handful of women in Montana who were willing to admit to anything. Unlike most of the local citizens — people who blame slippery politicians, incompetent lawyers, a bad mother, an unfaithful wife, an unfair world, anybody and everybody for their bigotry, everybody, of course, except themselves—I had already owned up to what I had done, all of it. Contrary to what was printed in the newspapers, most of the myths about me were untrue.

The newspapers fed everyone's imagination with news of the colored woman bigger than a man who dressed like a man, cursed like a man, drank whiskey like a man, and looked like a man, claiming this and that about me and the territories and the West. If what they were saying about me was so damned important to the history of the West, you would have thought the reporters could have at least bothered to get the facts right, and the same for the mayor. Did they get the facts straight? Not a prayer.

Sure, everyone agreed I was among the West's legends, a pioneer, a colored woman larger than life who insisted on respect, but where do we go from there? Mysteriously, nobody bothered to ask. So, I was ready to tell the reporter everything, to confess, to set the record straight.

I continued thinking back on my life, not merely to remember what happened, but to understand, really understand, how it all happened and *why*. I wasn't certain how long it would take to figure out the exact point in life when my soul drove me to challenge what society expected of a colored woman, when I began to match *crass behavior with crass behavior*. Maybe I remembered some of it wrong, but I wanted to share enough of the story with reporter so he could help me figure it out. It would be the first time my story got told right. I started off by mentioning how I helped Sister Amadeus at the Mission, including curing her of pneumonia.

Chapter Five

Montana Territory, November 1885

The Mission wasn't in Cascade. It was a ten-minute ride north of Cascade by two horse carriage. It took most men longer to hitch the team than it took for me to hitch the team and complete the entire trip.

I wouldn't call the land out there anything but wild. I could see the Cascade Mountains looming against the horizon in all directions, and during daylight hours, the sky seemed to sit down on the land and say howdy. The prairie was covered by brush, mangled trees, rocks, sand, and no sign of human habitation. The condition of the Mission was just as wild. It really wasn't a Mission at all.

There was no chapel or dormitories for the Blackfoot girls to gain a white woman's version of an education. Speaking bluntly, this is the reason the bishop felt it was so important for Sister Amadeus to blaze the trail to Montana. If the Blackfoot girls were given a white woman's education, they, at least in theory, would become mothers who would enforce the white man's concept of civilization on their children. This was part of Washington's grand design to make the Blackfeet less hostile to the Western expansion. However, it was clear that if the Blackfoot girls were going to receive a white woman's education, they would have to receive it at a tiny cluster of God-forsaken cabins. There was no traditional Mission here to speak of. Apparently, the resolve to build such a Mission, at least temporarily, exceeded the Ursuline Convent's capacity for missionary zeal.

The flaw in the theory that the Blackfeet could be tamed by indoctrination was the tiny group of cabins where the indoctrination was supposedly to have taken place. Three cabins with mud roofs were no match for forty below zero winter wind, blizzards, and drifting snow. The chapel, stone schoolhouse, and dormitories would not be built until much later.

Sister Amadeus, an asthmatic, was a petite woman. The combination of the bitter cold, the flimsy cabins, and her fragile constitution proved disastrous. She was deathly ill with pneumonia.

When I threw open her cabin door, she did not possess the strength to rise from her cot to greet me. She was near death.

The patchwork quilt over her tiny body resembled a funeral shroud. The flickering light in the gas lanterns made faint shadows dance against the logs on the one room cabin's walls. The rapidly dying fire in the field stone fireplace seemed literally to gasp for air. There were iron pots and pans, a table surrounded by several chairs with straw seats on a dirt floor.

The affairs of cooking, reading, writing, and sleeping that were once conducted in this room had been abandoned long ago. Sister Amadeus appeared only to be waiting for the inevitability of death. The normally rosy color of her face was gone. It was replaced by an ashen mask nearly as white as snow. The gold-edged pages of an open oversized Bible were on display over the fireplace.

The wind screamed outside, unimpressed by the coming of the darkness that is death. The cabin walls offered little resistance. The wind sounded nearly as loud inside the cabin as it sounded outside. It is not an overstatement to say death was waiting somewhere in that room, had blown straight into the place like the wind.

The nearest doctor was over sixty miles away in Helena. Instead of a doctor, an elderly nun wearing a black habit sat on a straw seat at Sister Amadeus's bedside. The nun attended to Sister Amadeus's body merely by working rosary beads. There was no medicine.

All that was left was Sister Amadeus's faith in the Risen Savior. I respected that same faith, the whiskey, the .38, the cursing, the brawling, and the rest of it aside. However, unlike the elderly nun at her bedside, I hadn't given up on the idea of boiling water and steam.

The elderly nun staked Sister Amadeus's health to the promise of faith and the power of prayer. Sister Amadeus, the picture of piety, seemed at peace with these methods, waiting. I wasn't.

"What in the living hell are you penguins doing?" I barked, slamming the door.

Startled by the intrusion, the nun at bedside cowered and shook. She stopped working the rosary beads.

"Who is this colored man?" the nun asked Sister Amadeus, defensively.

"Mary!" Sister Amadeus said, wheezing, coughing, gasping. Not bothering to correct the elderly nun's mistake, Sister Amadeus tried to sit upright, but failed.

This robbed her of what little air she had left in her lungs. She began to cough uncontrollably. She leaned over the edge of the bed. She spat at the floor.

The nun waited for an explanation.

"Mary?" asked the elderly nun, curiously.

"Yes, it is *my* Mary," Sister Amadeus said, coughing and

gasping. "She has come all the way from Ohio to save me. I do need saving, don't I?"

"Damn right you do. Now you, sister, step aside. Captain Death has visited this cabin, and I am here to send him back from whence he came."

I took the jar of whiskey I had hidden under my coat, unscrewed the lid, and took a belt of whiskey right there in front of the nuns. Then, I reached under my dress, produced the .38, and dropped it on the table. It wasn't fully loaded, but it got the nun's attention. I dropped a handful of bullets, too.

The nun stared at the spectacle in disbelief, but didn't dare speak. After I pulled off my coat, I realized how cold it was in the room.

"Damn, girls. It's too cold in here."

"We don't have much firewood left. We are saving it, nursing the fire," the elderly nun explained.

"What the hell are you saving the wood for? A funeral? Forget that! Bad idea. You go over to that fire and use as much wood as you have to get the fire roaring hotter than the blazing fires of Hell, understand?"

The nun didn't move.

"Now, dammit!" I barked.

The nun followed the command.

"Sister is dying," I whispered.

I slung my coat over the patchwork quilt on the bed, grabbed an axe and shotgun, and headed for the door.

"Where are you going?" asked the elderly nun, as she tossed wood on the gasping fire.

"I'm going to get firewood, where the hell do you think?"

"With no coat? You'll freeze to death. Besides, Father Damiani and Mother Stanislaus were already here days ago with the military doctor from Ft. Shaw. The doctor already treated Mother Amadeus. We have our instructions."

"I'm here to tell you those instructions are dead wrong. Keep that fire blazing. Make her sweat. I'll be back."

"Do you know how to treat pneumonia without a doctor?" the elderly nun asked.

"Does anyone?" I turned up the jar of whiskey, let the liquid burn as it reached my belly, and then I ventured to offer an explanation. "Do the doctors know how to treat pneumonia? I don't think so. Does anyone? The mortality rate for pneumonia is over sixty percent. If I have a sixty percent chance of dying by going to get a doc, well, hell, I can do that bad all by myself. Now, listen up, sister. I survived slavery in Tennessee, not because I was dumb or weak or stupid or anything of the sort, and not because I got put down by pneumonia, croup, dysentery, or alcohol. How many doctor's visits do you think you get on a slave plantation? Hmmm? You learn how to fight dysentery, croup, alcoholism, and pneumonia on your own. If you don't learn how to cheat death on your own, just who do you think will come along to help you? I'll be back." There was no answer.

I forced open the cabin door and met the howling wind and blinding snow.

I wasn't really sure I'd be back. However, I was sure that if I didn't make it back, I would die trying. The nun's words that I'd freeze to death were stuck in my mind.

I was new to these parts. I might not know where to find firewood in the middle of the sunshine on the finest summer day. The blinding snows of Montana at night would make it next to impossible. I didn't have a choice. Sister Amadeus was dying.

I was knee-deep in snow drifts. I couldn't see, and I wasn't wearing snow shoes. These weren't good odds. Nevertheless,

I kept going.

I tried to keep my sense of direction. If I got a good distance from the cabin, I would need to figure out how to get back, an unlikely proposition when you were caught in a blizzard. Those were the challenges—firewood, and the way back to the cabin. I soon would learn of a third challenge, a pack of wolves.

The wolves had taken an interest in my situation. I heard the yelping in the darkness. The yelping was closing in on me fast. I could hear it through the noise of the wind.

"Hey! Get!" I yelled at the darkness.

I kept looking into the darkness, until I could see the pack for the first time. It was on the move. The wolves must have smelled something on me, maybe it was the liquor or the scent of pork from the cabin.

The wolves leered, tongues lolling. They barked excitedly, jumping, turning themselves inside and out, but steadily approaching. When they arrived, the wolves eagerly stepped over each other, waiting to attack.

"I said, get! Get! Get going!"

There must have been a lead dog calling the shots, because the pack did not charge. It waited, tactically. The wolves didn't take a single, threatening step in my direction, not yet anyway.

The wolves merely watched, waited. The dogs cocked their heads as if to puzzle over the situation. They seemed to read the situation, watching, waiting to attack. They knew death was near. One wolf barked.

It must have been the lead dog. The bark was more like an assertion of dominance. I knew the pack was hungry. The dogs were undersized. They had few options. They needed food.

"Oh, so you want to play. Okay, let's play."

I cocked the shotgun. I fired. There was a yelp. I must have hit one of them. I fired a second shot for insurance. The wolves began barking excitedly, but did not flee.

I began climbing a hill to find higher ground. The pack yelped and snarled and growled after me. The wolves were a good twenty yards behind, but I could see the outline of the pack against the snow. I knew the dominant position was on higher ground. I ran, my feet clopping awkwardly. I could hear the snarling pack getting closer. I turned to face it, back-pedaling as I climbed, careful not to trip over the snow.

Suddenly, the wind and snow stopped. The clouds fled the sky, so the moon was showing. Now, I could see the pack clearly. It was made grey by the moonlight against the snow drifts. I could also hear the snarling.

The wolves were getting ready, planning the strike, the pounce. I still couldn't tell how many dogs were in the pack. They were running uphill towards me.

I triggered the shotgun. The blast seared through the pack, igniting panic. There was yelping and barking and pleading and confusion, and then the pack scattered, disappeared into the grey of the snow and the night.

"Good choice, you bastards. I got more lead on me, trust me."

I figured the wolf pack might return. If it did, the wolves would return in greater numbers. I had to prepare myself for the worse. It was the open prairie.

The sound of the wind returned, whispering, pleading. It wasn't a strong wind, the kind that makes it snow sideways. It was a gentle wind, the kind that reminds you it is in charge. I climbed higher.

I wasn't sure if the wolves would return. I discovered bare

apple trees on the hillside. The trees grow straight up there. I felt the trunks for moss. The moss grows on the north side of trees. I wanted to find North to orient myself.

Apple trees are hardwoods. I knew from my days on the plantation in Tennessee that hardwood trees are difficult to chop down, so I looked for dead branches. There were quite a number of fallen twigs and branches on the snow at the base of the trees. I gathered as many loose twigs and branches as I could into a pile. I tore part of my dress to make strips of cloth. I used the strips to tie the twigs and branches into bundles.

I started chopping anyway. The trunk was narrow, but the hardwood didn't chop easily. I had to lean into the axe handle to make any progress. When I put my full might into it, the wood chips began to fly. I worked and worked and finally got the tree to yield. It started to lean, but did not fall. I sent the final blows of the axe head into the wood.

Still, the tree would not fall. I pushed it the rest of the way over with my bare hands. Then, I chopped part of the trunk into precise sections. I split the sections into chunks. There was only a limited amount of wood I could carry in one load. I would return for more later.

I hauled two bundles, one with twigs and branches and the other with the logs I split. I didn't carry the bundles over my shoulders. I left them on the ground. I made a sled of cloth and dragged the firewood back to the cabin.

The cabin was hot. The elderly nun had followed instructions. The flames were leaping in the fireplace.

I dropped the wood on the dirt floor and screamed in pain.

"What's wrong?"

"Frostbite," I said.

"Frostbite?"

"Get me water. My fingers are swelling. I can't feel them.

There is so much pain."

"What?"

"Water!"

The nun brought a bucket of hot water.

"No, I need ice cold water! Dammit! Warm water will make it worse. You have to start with cold water and gradually bring my fingers back to body temperature with cold water," I said. "Hot water will cause the worse pain in the world."

The nun acquiesced. I immersed both hands in a pan of cold water.

"I have to put my hands in cold water. I hope the pain stops soon. I have to gradually get the temperature back in my hands. I can't feel nothing now. In the meantime, make Sister Amadeus tea. Wake her up. Make her drink."

The elderly nun was getting good at following instructions. She held the cup to Sister Amadeus's slips.

"Now, get a glass, put a couple of pinches of salt in warm water, and make the sister gargle and spit, even if she doesn't want to do it," I instructed.

The feeling was coming back to my fingers. The pain was going away. I got a pan of water that was standing at room temperature. I worked my fingers in the warm water. The feeling was coming back.

"I need ginger, peppermint, turmeric, and any other herb you got here. Got any here?" I asked to nobody in particular, as I searched, using my frostbitten fingers.

"We have peppermint candy and ginger in the jars on the shelf over there," said the elderly nun.

"Good, I will grind it up and make a strong medicinal tea."

I made the tea. I asked Sister Amadeus to drink. I dismissed the nun and stoked the fire myself. I fed wood to that fire all night. I wrapped an onion in a cloth and applied it Sister

Amadeus's chest. We were alone all night in that cabin.

Every time Sister Amadeus stirred under the quilt, I made her sit up and drink tea. The cabin was brutally hot. The quilt was wet with sweat.

I reassured Sister Amadeus that I would cut the fire before she drifted back to sleep. I lied. I wanted her to think that relief was near. The only thing that was near was death.

She coughed and spat.

She was weak with fever. She fell asleep again. I made the fire even hotter. We needed plenty of heat to get through the night. I knew she could sweat the devil out of her. I had seen it done back on the plantation. This battle went on all night.

By daybreak, the fever was gone.

Sister Amadeus sat up in her bed. The elderly nun returned. The elderly nun was shocked by the transformation. It was truly a miracle!

In the coming days, Sister Amadeus got stronger. There was less coughing and spitting. Then, there was none. Sister Amadeus was free of pneumonia!

I couldn't help but compare how my beloved Sister Amadeus's recovery from pneumonia felt similar to my liberation from slavery. We both had been given a second chance in life. We both were free.

I figured my work in Montana was done. I would return to Ohio. I thought it was wise to take Sister Amadeus back to Ohio, too.

She was asthmatic; she was frail; and she was possessed of historic missionary zeal, the zeal to bring the Heart of Jesus to all of Montana, including, with particularity, the children of the tribal nations. In other words, I knew the holy woman simply would not quit. Conversely, the wilds of Montana were unlikely to quit either, the sudden blizzards, the sub-zero temperatures, the drifting snow, the hungry winter wolves, all of it. This was not a good combination. Furthermore, I knew that if a nun so much as needed a needle and thread, not to mention food, supplies, and medical attention, she would need to hitch a team and suffer a two-day carriage ride to Helena to get it.

"Sister, this place is wild as all Hell. It is unsettled. What in the living Hell are we doing here? It is not safe to stay in this crazy wilderness, especially with you coughing and wheezing with asthma. The winters are full of blizzards and temperatures below zero. How long do you think it will be before you get a second bout of pneumonia? Let's just get a coach to Miles City, catch the Northern Pacific, and get the hell out of here. What do you say?"

Sister Amadeus didn't seem disturbed by the raw vulgarity of the plea. Instead, the soft spoken and eternally pious nun took my plea to the Risen Savior in prayer. The outcome was predictable.

"*Heko el hamsto*," she whispered.

"For Christ's sake, shit! I don't know what that means, but if I know you it is probably not good, it probably means no," I thought my saucy reply must have made even the Risen Savior's cheeks burn.

Sister Amadeus ignored my intemperate manner. She said in the king's English, "*Heko el hamsto* means, 'I stand firm like the mountains.'"

She further explained that she had been called to Montana by the Risen Christ. She would never forsake that calling, and the idea of failure was abhorrent to her. Speaking with authority as the Rev. Mother Amadeus of the Heart of Jesus, Foundress of the still unbuilt Ursuline Mission of Montana, she would never yield to the temptation to return to the comfort and safety of civilization in Ohio if it meant abandoning her Mission. She invited me to stay in Montana and help her build the Mission stone by stone. I could see the twinkle in this powerful Christian woman's eyes, and I knew her spirit was pure.

Sister Amadeus was known worldwide for her missionary zeal, patience, leadership, intellectual command, erudition, and, above all, her pureness of heart in the Christian faith. She was a giant. Her unique qualities would eventually allow her to do it all.

The faith she exhibited at the Ursuline Convent in Toledo would eventually lift her to extraordinary heights. She would establish a Convent in Miles City, Missions in Montana at Cascade and Tongue River, and a Mission in faraway Alaska. She was honored to be the first to receive the Holy Communion with a Flathead girl from Montana ahead of the multitudes at the Basilica in Rome. She evangelized the Blackfeet, Cheyenne, Sioux, Flathead, and Eskimos. She educated the daughters of mighty chiefs, like White Bull.

At the time, the railroads and telegraph wires had only recently begun to crisscross the prairies, and some tribal nations were still hostile to the United States agents and the ideal of the Western expansion. They still harbored mistrust for the "weo," which is Cheyenne for the "white man." As a writer, her eloquently composed letters were openly compared to the work of St. Theresa. Sister Amadeus was one of only a few distinguished religious figures to receive papal correspondence directly from Pope Benedict XV at the Vatican. She saw the Pacific Ocean at Coronado Beach. Indeed, she was among the prominent Jesuit missionaries credited with opening doors to the Western expansion. I knew that such a woman was unlikely to take no for an answer from the likes of me.

"Shit," I mumbled and agreed to stand by her side. "Before you know it, she'll have me wearing a full buckskin suit, dammit."

Buckskin suit aside, the two of us, Sister Amadeus and a formerly enslaved colored woman standing six feet tall, would come to confront the perilous wilds of Montana together, the blizzards, the sub-zero temperatures, the hungry winter wolves, the bandits, the hostile Indians, all of it. The reason was simple. Our bond of friendship was indelible, possibly indomitable. Why not? It had already cheated death. What could the snarling teeth of a hungry wolf pack possibly do to threaten our resolve? However, the question of whether our resolve would withstand the rigors of building a stone Mission with scant resources and little, if any, dependable help was quite a separate matter.

The work of transforming the cluster of cabins into a real Mission, one with a stone chapel, a bell, and a flagpole, one with dormitories and a legitimate schoolhouse, hadn't even begun. There was no garden or henhouse. There wasn't even a stable for the horses. The Mission was a pathetic cluster of cabins with mud floors in the middle of an open field. The weeds had even taken root on the mud roofs.

The Mission needed a foreman to oversee the transformation. The Church would look to hire someone with a whole range of skills from carpentry, masonry, gardening to tending the horses, standing watch over the grounds, and warding off random attacks by hungry wolves, hostile Sioux, drunken Irishmen, and Mexican *banditos*. Even with helpers, wagons, and mules, the work of carrying building stones from nearby Square Battle Quarry to the Mission would be arduous. It was a tall order, indeed. In short, it was considered a man's work. Sister Amadeus had other ideas. She had her mind set on still another miracle.

Chapter Six

The draft snatched at Father Damiani's black robes as he walked purposely from his cabin across the open field to Sister Amadeus's cabin. The way the wind clawed at the priest's robes was precisely the same way it had clutched at Sister Amadeus's lungs that winter.

We spent the entire winter alone together in that cabin. It was now spring. The priest suspected all along that Sister Amadeus and I were more than just good friends. He believed we were actually lovers. Now, he was determined to catch us in the act.

Father Damiani banged furiously at the cabin door.

"Open up, open up this minute," he demanded.

"Yes, what is it?" Sister Amadeus said, opening the door slowly.

Sister Amadeus, as an Ursuline nun, was known as the "Spouse of the Crucified." She was fully dressed in her habit, including tunic, belt, scapular, and veil. She was fresh and ready for the day's work to begin. The habit made it easy to see why the Indians called the Ursuline nuns the "Black Gowns." In concert with the Christian faith, she refused to judge the priest for the wrongful accusation or the indiscretion. On the other hand, I did.

I didn't wear black. It wasn't one of my favorite colors. Instead, I wore a white apron over a floor length grey dress.

Unlike Sister Amadeus, I wasn't ready for the day's work to begin. I couldn't care less what Father Damiani thought of our situation. So, I lounged on a chair before the cabin's open window, puffing away on a homemade black cigar.

"What's going on in here?" the priest said, neglecting to close the door.

The priest had arrived from Helena the night before and had been told of my immense physique, but coming face to face with it startled him.

"Close the damned door." I blew a puff of blue smoke. "Were you raised in a barn?" I said, not bothering to put out the cigar. I was already liquored up, having thrown up a flask of whiskey a time or two at sunrise.

"You will refrain from using vulgarity while on church premises," the priest said, sheepishly.

"I told her the exact same thing," Sister Amadeus agreed.

"I'll give you the same answer," I interrupted. "I'm not a slave. I am through with slavery, thanks to Mr. Lincoln. I will say whatever I please to whoever I please wherever I please whenever I please. What, do you think the Indian girls here will mind? They barely speak English."

I felt slighted. The priest seemed to have very little regard for exactly how sick Sister Amadeus had been or the enormity of the miracle that was needed to save her. I felt unappreciated. I had come all the way to the Mission by stagecoach, performed the miracle of restoring Sister Amadeus's health and saved the Mission's founder, its Mother Superior, and I planned to leave Montana in the spring the same way I had arrived, by stagecoach.

"Jesus will mind," the priest said.

"Here we go with that shit again," I said.

"Shhhh," Sister Amadeus insisted.

"Hell, why do you have a Mission for Blackfoot Indian girls anyway? Why teach Blackfoot Indians English out in the middle of Godforsaken Montana? Do you want to make them translators? If Jesus knows everything, don't you think he's figured that one out, too?" I was upset and drunk.

"We teach them English, madam, so they can read the Bible," the priest said, confidently.

"Why not simply write the Bible in Blackfoot, mister, and call it a day. That way they can read it on their own?" I chuckled.

"Let's not have a debate," Sister Amadeus said.

"There will be no debate," the priest said.

"Mary helped me get over my sickness. She's visiting. We grew up together back on my family's plantation," Sister Amadeus said.

"She will refrain from vulgarity or I'm afraid this little visit will be canceled, and the medicine bought to you by the military doctor from Ft. Shaw more than likely deserves the credit," the priest said.

"There's plenty she can do for us. She's an excellent carpenter, gardener, blacksmith, cook, coachman, and we have a need for all five," Sister Amadeus said.

"Five?" I laughed. "That sounds more like fifty-five."

"Coach*man*?" the priest said, placing emphasis on the word "man." "This is no man. You came all the way here by coach from where?" the priest asked.

"Toledo, Ohio,"

"And you have the audacity to call Montana Godforsaken?"

"She can harness a team faster than any man, swing a hammer better than any man, travel by horseback farther, fight better…" Sister Amadeus said, excitedly.

"Fight better?" the priest said, curiously. "How on earth would one know that?" he asked, mumbling.

"That, too," I said.

"Curse better, too, I'll bet," the priest said. "Well, she is certainly bigger than any man in Cascade. I can tell you that, so I'll put it to the test. I have interviews set up for this afternoon to add a foreman to the staff to run our projects. Albert, who is our only hired helper, is only a janitor. We have a need to build a school, and I have to send the wagon regularly to pick up supplies. I'll tell you what: I have a competition set up for this afternoon to see which man in town can harness and hitch a two-horse team to a coach the fastest. It is a real test of skill. That seems like the fairest way to decide who gets the job. Albert will try, and if he wins, he gets a promotion. If someone else wins, they get the job. I'll let your Mary, here, enter, and if she wins, she'll get the job, but the chances of her beating a man out here in Montana are dim—dim, indeed."

"Perfect," Sister Amadeus said.

"I'll win," I said, dismissively.

The priest closed the door, and when he did, I turned up the flask I had been hiding beneath my apron, took another slug of whiskey, and saluted the spot at the door where the priest had been standing. "And it's a good thing I'll win. The goddamned place is falling apart. I mean there are weeds literally growing on the roof."

Chapter Seven

There were two men set to compete, three men if you counted me. I might as well have been a man standing there in the dust and the wind and the sun outside the grounds of St. Peter's Mission waiting for the priest's contest to begin.

There were three empty carriages standing in a perfect line. The work horses were grazing at the edge of the dirt road that ran past the Mission and all the way into town. The harnesses, bridles, collars, yokes, and a tangle of leather straps were in piles on the ground. I was a head taller and at least fifty pounds heavier than each of my competitors.

The work horses seemed oblivious to the drama that was about to unfold. They had heavy faces. They snorted, blew, and tossed their heads as they grazed on the very open field the Catholics hoped would one day become a lawn. Actually, the only creatures moving that day that were taller than me were the horses.

The men would have to look up to find the horses' withers and hurriedly throw the harnesses over their backs in order to win the contest. On the other hand, I was tall enough to look the horses directly in the eye and look down on their sway backs as I tossed the harnesses over the backs of my team.

The men waited for the priest to appear out of the shadows of the Mission, open the gate, and start the competition. The men avoided eye contact with me. Nevertheless, I stared at them. I wanted to intimidate them.

"Which of you boys is coming in second?" I asked. "This ain't gonna be no real competition. I'm fixing to kick your asses. This is going to be an exhibition, an ass kicking exhibition, not a contest. Hell, you boys don't look like you know your way around a horse and know even less about running a coach."

I watched the eyes of the men. They didn't look at me. Instead, the men looked at the ground.

"Talk a lot of shit, lady." Albert, the shorter of the two men, finally mustered courage. He was a short Mexican with black, oily hair. He had a barrel chest, like he hadn't missed many meals.

The taller of the two men, a slender Irishman with a long, ruddy nose, didn't say anything. He put his hands in his pockets and looked at the ground.

"There ain't nothing much written on the ground there that you're staring at that is likely to help you any now, do you think?" I taunted.

The priest emerged from the shadows of the Mission. His black robes twirling in the wind seemed hideous outside on the open field with the prairie all around. I guess that's where the folks in Cascade got the idea to call the priests at the Mission "Black Robes." The wind had its way with his hair, too.

There was a silver crucifix dangling from a long chain around the priest's neck. The jewelry was quite impossible to miss. A group of Ursuline nuns followed, the points of their veils made them look like a flock of birds with wings poised for flight. Their Mother Superior, Sister Amadeus, followed the group into the sunlight. She, too, was excited over the promise of the contest.

The tangle of black leather straps, chains, rings, collars,

yokes, and other equipment in each pile on the ground would likely be nearly impossible to untangle quickly, or at all, particularly if you didn't know exactly how to harness and hitch horses. The priest had purposely rigged the piles to test our skill. The contest was designed to test both skill and speed. In this way, the race would resemble the steamboat race between the Robert E. Lee and Natchez.

There were massive collars that had to be placed over each horse's neck and shoulders. The harnesses, including brass hames, spider, hip drops, breachings, turnbacks, tug chains, quarter straps, girth bands, belly bands, butt straps, bottom hames straps, and bridles, including bits, tongue chains, reins, and blinders, had to be sorted, arranged, thrown over the backs of the beasts, and cinched, and then the team of two horses had to be backed into position to hitch the whole affair to the shaft of the coach. This was a handful. The whole operation took the finest coachmen over ten minutes to complete. I doubted the Mexican and the Irishman could figure out the riddle if they were given an hour head start.

"Silence," the priest said, raising his right hand. "Get ready, set…go!"

He dropped his right hand.

The contestants sprinted to the piles. The nuns cheered loudly, pulling for their favorite contestant, almost as though the pious nuns had taken odds and staked wagers on which of the contestants would prevail. They rooted hard, pounding their fists, stamping their feet, and hollering, like the crowds that gather near the quarter pole at Churchill Downs as horses turn for home in the Kentucky Derby.

The contestants hauled the mass of leather straps, chains, and other equipment to where the horses grazed, leather straps trailing behind comically. They dropped the piles on the ground, picked them up again, only to see the leather straps and chains spill hopelessly over their arms in a tangle. The process of untangling the mess was underway.

The men puzzled over the leather straps and chains, comically turning them upside down, right side up, holding them up, dropping them, stepping on them, and cursing at them. Conversely, I coolly and expertly spread my pile on the ground, sorting the leather straps, chains, and other equipment into a logical sequence, separating the bridle from the harness, and ordering the entire affair. I even stopped to light a cigar. I held the cigar between my teeth as I worked. Cigar smoke trailed overhead.

I hefted the first ordered pile and carried it to the two horses that would form my team. I fit the collar over the head and neck of the right-side horse. The horse accepted the collar on its shoulders without incident. The horses stood proudly erect for me, like statues. Then, I threw the collar on the left-side horse and asked it to line up alongside the right-side horse.

"Whoa, now back to me, now back to me, back to me," I said.

The horse followed the mysterious commands as though we shared a secret language. "Now, get over there, get over, get over there."

The horse side stepped, inched slowly, and side stepped again until my team stood side by side perfectly. "Now stand!" The horses obeyed. It was magnificent. It was fast.

Still confounded, the Mexican and the Irishman held the straps of their piles hopelessly in the air. They tried to figure out which strap and which chain went where in the configuration.

I ignored them. I was tall enough to see over the withers of my horses. I threw the harness, including the framework of leather straps and chains, over the back of the right-side horse. The hames was adjusted so that it sat snuggly in a groove on top of the collar. I proceeded to adjust and cinch the quarter strap, girth band, belly band, butt strap, and spider, swinging low beneath the horse's belly when necessary, puffing my black cigar when necessary, too. Once again, I was outrageously overconfident.

I dropped the bridle over the horse's head with expert precision, opening the horse's rubbery lips so it would accept the bit, cinched the straps, and pulled the reins to the left-hand side of the horse. With the bulk of the equipment's framework on the right-hand side of the right horse, I dropped the reins to the ground on the left and commanded: "Now, stand." The right-side horse complied.

The nuns cheered.

The nuns laughed and pointed as the clumsy inefficiency of the Mexican and the Irishman was on full display. The Mexican stared at the tangle of straps in the pile like it was calculus. The Irishman dragged his somewhat orderly pile to his horses, trying to catch up to me. In a way, he was catching up. In another way, he was hopelessly far behind.

The Irishman threw the collars on his team. He was catching up. The Mexican was hopelessly far behind in third place, still fumbling with leather straps.

I repeated the process of throwing the harness over the back of the left-side horse that I had completed with the right-side horse, adjusting the bridle, cinching the straps, bands, and chains in precisely the same fashion as I had done with the right-side horse, except I dropped the reins on the right side of the horse when I was finished, and the bulk of the equipment was on the outer left side of the left-side horse. I crossed the reins through a brass ring between horses. Now, I was ready to hitch the team to the sled. I was almost finished.

I let out the full length of the reins and held the thin leather straps between my horses far away from their rumps. Then, I began to walk them backwards methodically.

"Now, back to me, back to me, back to me," I said, calling to the horses.

The team responded, inching slowly backwards together as a team. The backward march continued until the horses had backed up to the coach, and the shaft of the coach was between them on the ground.

"Whoa, stand," I commanded, tying off the reins on the coach.

The Irishman had his harness and bridle in place on his right-side horse. The right-side horse was ready to be hitched. He only needed to harness the left-side horse of his team to catch up to me. However, this didn't trouble me at all: I remained composed, unaffected, even manly.

I calmly walked around to the front of the team, picked up the iron bar and ran the bar through the ring in the shaft. I was in full command, even dismissive of the competition. I walked calmly to the rear of the team, hooked chains on each side of each horse to the sled, and climbed aboard the coach to tie off the reins.

When I hopped off the coach, my team stood proud, obedient, and motionless, like magnificent statues. I was the victor. It wasn't even close.

The men still fiddled hopelessly, comically, with the straps and chains. This went on for another twenty minutes in the case of the Irishman, and the Mexican's case was hopeless. He was relieved of his trouble by the priest. It was clear that he had no idea what he was doing and would never figure out the puzzle of leather straps, chains, and special equipment. There was no reason to prolong the agony.

The nuns talked openly about the competition now that it was over, nearly one-half hour after it had begun, and nearly twenty minutes after I had already beaten both of my male competitors. The priest formally announced that I had indeed won. My team was harnessed, hitched, and ready, but I was gone.

The nuns searched everywhere to congratulate me on winning the race, everywhere, that is, except where I was hiding. They looked inside cabins, behind trees and bushes, behind cabins, nearly everywhere. Finally, I was discovered sitting under the sprawling branches of a shade tree, turning up a whiskey flask, smoking a cigar, outrageously confident.

Chapter Eight

I won the job of Mission foreman. This empowered me to perform what seemed like an endless string of miracles at the Mission. I built the fieldstone chapel, steeple, bell tower, schoolhouse, dormitory, and stables. There were flagpoles, a hen house, and a garden. I instituted a system of bells at the Mission, seven bells for breakfast in the morning, twelve bells for lunch, five bells for dinner, three bells for danger, and nine bells for lights out at night.

I taught the cooks how to prepare my special tea to cure sicknesses, like pneumonia, whooping cough, and dysentery. I built a chicken coup and raised chickens, so the Mission had fresh eggs in the morning. I patched the thatched roof of the Mission, replaced windows, and even taught classes of Blackfoot girls how to read and write when the nuns were ill. I drove a team of horses on supply runs to the general store in town. I supervised the Mexican, training him in the trades, and the two of us began to build a new school using the funds that trickled into the Mission from the priest's connections with the Church.

I served as security guard as well. My black skin and daunting size puzzled the Indians, outlaws, wolves, and black bears that had once made sport out of raiding the Mission. And when my daunting size wasn't an adequate deterrent, I had the ten-gauge shotgun and the .38 to fall back on. Even the priest admitted I was sent from heaven.

The priest said wealthy financiers were building a railroad, and it was coming to Helena and Great Falls. The bishop predicted the railroad would not only bring prosperity to the Territory, but it would also bring even more outlaws and trouble. The town wasn't officially incorporated until 1887, and the railroad depot opened the next year. The rumors of gold and the cattle drives from overcrowding in Texas to the open grassy plains of the Pacific Northwest guaranteed action. There was little doubt of the value of a woman with a hulking frame to an isolated Mission in the wilds of the Montana Territory.

If all of this wasn't enough, I even cut the grass on the Mission's lawn, and I was known to curse at whoever walked across freshly cut grass, whether it was a student, a nun, or even the bishop himself. I became so beloved that the Mission made a tradition of celebrating my birthday on March 15th, though, as a formerly enslaved woman, I was never quite sure of my actual date of birth. Although the Mission was preoccupied with the Gospel, I clung to my proclivities: I cursed, smoked cigars, and drank whiskey, and I was willing to do so unapologetically whenever I pleased, which was on a daily basis.

I drank so much whiskey that I managed to break the gender line at the local saloon. I was the first and only woman not working as a prostitute ever allowed in the saloon to drink whiskey in Montana Territory, and I drank whiskey often, brawled often, cursed often, and gambled often. This was perhaps the first instance of a woman receiving equal treatment with a man in the entire Territory. My "crass behavior" superseded the narrow prejudices of the time and planted the idea in their heads that narrow prejudices against women were just that, narrow. Ironically, I was working at the Mission at the same time that I frequented the saloon.

Chapter Nine

The snow drifts were over six feet high. Some of the drifts even swept over the Mission roofs. That wasn't necessarily a bad thing. The snow drifts insulated the cabins, like warm blankets. I piled plenty of snow against the logs at the bottom of the outside walls of each building and piled plenty of firewood at the fieldstone fireplaces, and I kept those fires burning, for pneumonia was a constant guest in Montana.

I was skillful at handling the brutality of winter. The idea of forty below zero was a way of life. The truth was, most folks in Montana were good at it. If you weren't, you simply froze to death. If you got your fingers or toes frostbitten, or heard a story about some fellow who got liquored up at the Silver Dollar saloon and froze to death on his way home, you began to get smart about survival.

The storm stopped overnight, leaving nothing but bright sunshine in the morning. The sun made you want to forget we were in the middle of a Montana winter. I had to hitch the team and ride to Helena to pick up supplies. Helena was a good two day's ride under these conditions and possibly into the next day through all of this snow.

Fortunately, I had a set of snow shoes. I used them to track on top of the snow drifts, and, of course, I had whiskey, a repeating rifle, and the .38. I found warmth and comfort in men's clothing, a wool hat pulled down over my ears with a bowler hat stacked on top of the wool hat for style, two enormous coats, a wool scarf wrapped loosely over each shoulder, two layers of wool britches, and leather shoes with laces. In this getup, standing at six feet tall with a broad back, enlarged hands, and a cigar, it would have been quite impossible to detect that I was a woman. That suited me fine. We were bound to attract the interest of bandits along the way.

Fortunately, we didn't experience any problems on the run to Helena. The team braved the going over snow drifts, bowing their necks proudly, twitching their ears alertly, dismissing the challenge of the treacherous going, kicking their knees over the snow with authority. I screamed over the singing brass harnesses and snapped the reins whenever I got the sense the horses began to lose their focus and puffed away on my cigar.

We arrived in Helena and purchased supplies, ham sides, bacon fat, sacks of beans and flour, coffee, tea, candy, kegs of molasses, and a bottle of whiskey. The Mission's credit was good in Helena, so I didn't settle the bill. I loaded the freight onto the wagon bed. It smelled sweet, like any load of fresh coffee, pork, and dry goods was expected to smell.

If it can be said that the run to Helena was uneventful, the return trip was quite the opposite. First, with little appreciation for my gender, I was allowed to sit in the Magnolia Saloon in Helena, drink whiskey, and wait for nightfall. I really don't believe anyone in the saloon was even aware that I was a woman, and I was never opposed to the idea of getting liquored up before hitching the team and setting off on a long run.

Unlike Cascade, the saloons in Helena were always too busy and too crowded to pay close attention to any particular customer, unless you called attention to yourself. Owned by a well-heeled German immigrant who belonged to the Masonic Temple, the bar at the Magnolia was surprisingly elegant.

The gas light chandeliers bathed the long room in dim light. The dim light, the elegance, the polished furniture, the steady flow of alcohol, the men busy working to impress one or more of the high-priced prostitutes in the room, the laughing, and the drinking seemed to have everyone on their best behavior. I suppose in a crowded saloon nobody bothered to inquire whether it was necessary to discriminate against me on the basis of gender, and I wasn't inclined to invite the inquiry by announcing my gender. I was on my best behavior, too.

I might have been mistaken for just another colored man passing through town or a rancher's hired hand, or quite possibly everyone was having too good a time to bother to care. This meant I had little difficulty buying shots of whiskey and throwing them down, one after the other.

Waiting for nightfall at the Magnolia before beginning a journey with a load of supplies on an open wagon was typically not a good plan. Furthermore, getting liquored up to do so wasn't a particularly good idea either. Second, the scent of the pork let every wild beast of the field in the vicinity know we were on our way. The confluence of these bad ideas proved disastrous.

I slapped the team with the reins, and we were off. It didn't take long for us to clear the bustle of Helena's busy main street. We were off in the open of the lonely prairie again.

As soon as we were an appreciable distance out of Helena, maybe two hours or so, it happened. The scent of pork attracted a pack of ravenous wolves. It was a particularly brutal winter. The food supply was scarce. I understood the issue. The wolves were interested in getting at the pork.

Out of the darkness, the wolves attacked. They weren't wolves anything like the ones I had confronted back in Cascade. These wolves meant business.

Suddenly, there was vicious barking and snarling. The horses screamed and reared. I grabbed the rifle.

The horses reared. The wolves barked and growled, and the growling was coming from more than one angle at the same time. The wolves were swarming, attacking with exposed teeth.

I got off a shot into the air. The commotion threw the front wheels of the wagon airborne. I held on to my rifle. The wagon wheels crashed to the ground. The weight of the freight shifted.

I fired a second wild shot. The blast cracked across the open prairie. I was careful not to aim downward. I didn't dare aim at the pack of wolves nipping at the panicked horses. I didn't want to risk hitting the horses.

With the second gunshot, the horses reared straight up in the air. This time the team objected in earnest. The horses thrashed wildly at the air with their front hooves while balancing on their hind legs. They were standing straight up in the air. Their heads and front legs were easily twelve feet above the attack on the ground. If the horses clipped one another with those sharp hooves, they would have cut each other wide open.

The wild white of the horses' eyes flashed in terror. Their front legs flailed. One of the wolves must have sent sharp teeth into the slender canon bones of at least one of the horses. I heard the pain and terror in the screams.

I triggered another shot. The report echoed. The horses whinnied and screamed.

The wolves didn't abandon the attack.

The gunshot did little, if anything, to dissuade the pack.

The pack was driven by the brutality of raw hunger. There was no fear. There could be no fear. It was Montana in winter. Fear counted for nothing. The only thing between the wolves and death was the pork onboard the wagon.

The desperate dogs bit, snarled, and circled. The horses stomped and panicked. There was desperation everywhere. The dogs were desperate for pork. I was desperate to escape. The horses were desperate to free themselves of the chaos.

The horses would have bolted if it wasn't for the harnesses, leather straps, and reins tethering them to the wagon. One of the horses started to buck. Who could blame it? The wolves were after our precious freight.

The horses reared yet again, lifting the front wheels of the wagon into the air. Both horses began bucking wildly, hoping to land the might of sharp hooves on wolf flesh.

I broke off a round straight up into the air. I still couldn't risk shooting the horses, but I had to reply. I had to repel the attack.

I triggered the rifle again and again with the barrel pointed skyward.

In the burst of adrenalin, it felt like I got off fifty shots. The reality is I was holding a Winchester. It was a sleek enough repeating rifle, but the magazine didn't have the capacity to hold fifty cartridges.

I recalled loading exactly ten cartridges when I rode out of Helena. I was liquored up at the time I did the loading, but the fog of alcohol didn't throw me off that much. In a split second, I counted seven cartridges left in the magazine.

The horses reared again. This time the front wagon wheels were thrown into the air. The horses thrashed and twisted to free themselves of the harnesses and leather straps. This sent the wagon into an odd motion.

The wagon wheels and wagon bed kicked sideways. I was thrown off the wagon. The wagon overturned. The supplies spilled onto the ground. The wolves tore into the supplies. This started a feeding frenzy.

This may have been a blessing. It gave me a clear shot at the pack. I fired. The pack scattered.

One of the wolves must have snagged a ham butt in its teeth, because the pack began to attack a single wolf. I could hear the wolves fighting among themselves in the darkness. The horrible sound of screaming and snarling and growling was hideous. With the spoils of the attack in its midst, the pack dashed away across the prairie. The attack was over.

I reloaded. I cocked the shotgun under one armpit, placed my right index finger along the trigger guard, and steadied the horses with my free hand. I didn't bother struggling to right the overturned wagon. That would come later.

I readjusted the bridles, careful to keep my shotgun at the ready. I inspected the mouths of the horses for cuts, keeping an eye on the darkness for signs of the pack. There were no cuts. I worked my hands over the canon bones, checking for indications of injuries. Miraculously, there were none.

With the team accounted for, I turned to the supplies. I stacked the bags of coffee and flour. They were still dry. The rest of the freight was in order. Aside from the ham butt, the only loss was one keg of molasses. It cracked when the wagon was overturned. Otherwise, we were surprisingly unscathed. It was indeed a miracle.

I decided I needed light to fix the wagon. Daybreak was only an hour or so away. However, I knew the pack would return. It had to return. Its survival depended on it. The freight would make for a meal too enticing to resist.

I decided to crack open the bottle of whiskey and stand guard. I lit a gas lantern and stood it on the ground. I shouldered the shotgun and waited.

After a while, I thought I saw a lone wolf. I didn't want to discharge the weapon and traumatize the horses. So, I decided to get close to the ground and watch.

"You sonofabitch think you are getting near this wagon, well, you got another think coming. I'll be bringing your pelt back to the Mission as a trophy, every last one of you pups. Hey! Hey! Get!"

There was no barking or yelping, so there was no need to trigger the rifle. There was only darkness. I waited. I lit a cigar and waited.

I fantasized that Sister Amadeus would be impressed that I could survive a wolf attack and return the team, wagon, and supplies in one piece, unscathed. I so wanted to please her. I looked forward to receiving adulation upon my return to the Mission.

"You sonsabitches have met your match," I said to the darkness. "This was one miraculous display of manhood, er, I mean, womanhood. You met your match. Now, you have your meal. *Nothing* is your meal. Eat nothing for your meal and like it." Surprisingly, the pack did not return.

There would be no meal for the wolves that night. Instead, there was despair and the beaten hardness of the earth and the bitter cold of winter in Montana.

The sun was at the rim of the Cascades in the morning. I started to attend to the overturned wagon. I spun the wagon wheels that were in the air. There was no damage.

I checked the wagon wheels under the weight of the overturned wagon. There was no damage there, either.

I laid down the rifle and pushed and heaved and forced the wagon upright. Sure, I could have waited for a wagonful of men to come along and help right the load, but that would have entailed a wait of hours. I wanted to return the supplies to the Mission *post haste*. I was eager to tell the story and receive the adulation.

Upon my return to the Mission, the nuns and girls spilled out of the schoolhouse to meet me. Their day was well underway. They worried that I had been overtaken by bandits along the return trip from Helena. I proudly told the story of the wolf attack to a rapt audience. It was still another story that pushed my life and times to legendary status.

Sure, I received adulation from the Blackfoot girls and the nuns, but the bishop presented an entirely different take altogether. He had already become suspicious. A flurry of complaints had already crossed his desk. Each complaint involved my "crass behavior." Liquor was the one constant in all of the complaints. He doubted the truth of my story about the wolf attack. He suspected intoxication was the real reason for the overturned wagon. Therefore, while I had displayed courage repelling the wolf attack, he displayed audacity by docking my pay for the one cracked keg of molasses I lost during the attack.

Sister Amadeus delivered news of the bishop's decision to me. The bishop figured supposition was an adequate substitute for evidence. I may have been drunk. I was typically drunk. Why on earth would anyone hold that against me? What did drunkenness have to do with the wolves? Nothing. This didn't stop the bishop from concluding otherwise and docking my pay.

The first thing I looked to do when I got news that my pay had been docked was go to the Silver Dollar and knock out the first rancher who owed me money. In other words, I was going to town looking to raise a little hell, to get even.

Chapter Ten

I promised myself I would make the first rancher I met in the saloon that day who owed me money and regaled me with a bogus story instead of simply settling his debt pay for what the bishop did to me.

I had been taking odd jobs outside of the Mission for quite some time prior to 1887, including earning extra money to go on supply runs, babysit, do laundry, help ranchers raise barns and houses, dig holes, fight Indians, really anything. It didn't matter what they asked me to do. I could do it all.

I had a huge heart, so I was lenient where it came to collecting what people owed me. However, if leniency was mistaken for weakness, or if I got enough whiskey in me, an entirely different Mary Fields would emerge, and all of the locals knew it. That might have been the reason I earned my reputation for "crass behavior," as they put it.

The Sioux called me White Crow for a reason. They said I acted like a white person in black skin. I wasn't exactly sure what they meant, or why anyone would say a thing like that just because I insisted on folks respecting my rights. However, it was already clear that I was blazing a trail of sorts in the Montana Territory. If Mary Fields had the right to sit in a saloon, drink whiskey, curse, fight, and do whatever else she pleased, why shouldn't other women be allowed to do the same?

In this respect, Mary Fields, all six feet and two hundred

pounds of me, including skin that was as black as the "burnt prairie," regardless of some of the unflattering nicknames I collected along the way, would eventually be hailed as a pioneer for women's rights. In fairness, it wasn't only that I looked like a man and packed a .38 that made me a pioneer of the Old West. Those weren't the only things that stood out.

If you stopped to think about it—really think about it—my appeal also included time and the beaten hardness of the earth and the pull of how the prairie against the Cascades seems magnificent in the morning sunlight when the sky is high and deep and all around and how the Western expansion revealed the inherent glory of the land and the inherent dignity of human rights. The audacity to insist on respect, and equal treatment, was the thing that folks in Cascade admired most about me. The reason they admired this quality is because it allowed them to see a lot of themselves in me.

Generally speaking, audacity is what made the Old West tick, and audacity was the part of me that was akin to folks out in Montana and everywhere else actually. Audacity doesn't need an introduction. Folks recognize it when they see it.

Looking back, audacity is what clicked with the folks of Cascade, and audacity pinpointed what made the nation great as a whole in the 1880s, made it evolve, made it feel confident to dream big and expand westward. Audacity is what the world admired about the Old West, the gunplay, the squatters, the ranchers, the farmers, the cattle rustlers, the bank and stagecoach robbers, the relentless will to brave cruel winters, the courage to just keep going west no matter the odds and no matter the obstacles, all of it boiled down to audacity. Audacity describes the spirit of the Old West better than all of the other words put together.

Audacity is the quality historians bump into when they are

trying to make sense of it all. Audacity built the railroads. Audacity possessed Mr. Lincoln to insist upon change, and audacity possessed the South to resist. Audacity encouraged former slaves to rise up and confront their captors. Audacity rushed for gold. Mary Fields, and the Old West, had plenty of audacity.

However, the local citizens who believed audacity would have saved them if they owed me money and visited a certain saloon in Cascade, Montana on the day after the bishop docked my pay would have been dead wrong. I was beyond pissed.

Cascade was still an unincorporated town at the time. The Territorial Legislative Assembly still had not passed the act incorporating it, creating offices to be filled, and Harvey Hill still hadn't been elected mayor. The rascal, who was obviously neither Republican nor of sound mind, hadn't yet misused his authority as mayor to place a ban on women entering saloons, a slight aimed directly at my "crass behavior." Later, my popularity became so overwhelming that not only was the ban reversed, but the locals would begin to celebrate my birthday each year. However, that is getting way ahead of the story.

Tom's Saloon in Cascade was not much to brag about. It was little more than a spiffy log cabin on a dusky street. There was glass in its one window. There was a tattered canopy over the front door.

Inside, the saloon wasn't much to talk about, either. There was a short bar, not one of the polished wooden bars that resembled fine furniture I admired in the Magnolia in Helena, but what you'd expect a poor excuse for a bar in a poor excuse for a town to look like. It was made of rough-hewn boards that hadn't received the dignity of wood stain or lacquer. There were wooden chairs and tables scattered about at random.

The saloon's patrons supposedly disarmed themselves at the door as a testament to the honor code that applied to saloons on the prairie. The rifles and shotguns that leaned against the wall was all the proof anyone seemed to need. The standup piano was rarely used. There was a map of the Pacific Northwest on one of the walls. There was always action, gambling, whiskey, prostitution, even though the prostitutes were usually the same ladies over and over.

You got the sense the earth was exposed just below the floorboards, because the boards sagged underfoot. I never let on what I really felt about the place. Nobody did. It was home, and I could throw back whiskey, strike up a conversation, and pass the time away there. What else was there to want out of life? Later, after I got good and liquored up, it would make sense to make some poor unsuspecting soul pay for the injustice the bishop visited on me.

There was a negro piano player wearing a bowler with a fancy satin hat band. You could hear the jumpy tune out in the street. I tied off my horse at the hitching rail and stepped inside.

"Hey, what's the occasion?" I asked, referring to the music.

"Huh?" the bartender asked.

"What's the occasion?" I screamed above the music.

"Got new girls coming in today from Helena," said the bartender.

"New girls, well yippy damned do! Boy, I tell you, hot damn!" I laughed.

"Yes, indeed, hot damn," the bartender agreed.

This wasn't the bartender who greeted me on my first day in Cascade. That fellow was long gone, back East. This fellow was part of the new guard in town that respected the rights of Mary Fields. He set me up with a shot of whiskey.

"What time you expecting the girls?"

"Why do *you* want to know *that*, Mary? You want to get you one yourself?"

There was a blast of laughter.

"Might be able to do more with one of them gals if I got one myself then all of you boys put together, who knows?" I said, luring him into the trap of trading wits with me.

"No doubt," said the bartender, declining the offer.

"Mary," yelled one of the ranchers at the end of the bar, "you're blacker than the prairie after it gets burnt out by a brush fire on a windy day. How exactly would you expect to get one of them gals anyway?"

There was laughter yet again.

"Same way you do, I suppose: Money," I retorted.

There was triumphant laughter. I had held my own on rebuttal. I was one of the town's favorite citizens.

"Well, what you figuring on getting them with, Mary?" the rancher persisted. "Which side do you keep *it* on anyway, the left side or the right side?"

"If by *it*, you mean the .38, don't bother asking where I keep it unless you want to find out firsthand."

The bartender set me up with another shot of whiskey.

However, I didn't have time to drink it. I spotted a hired man wearing a Stetson who hadn't paid his laundry bill with me. He was passing the bar on the street. I saw him through the glass window. I ignored the whiskey. I set out of the bar after him.

"Hey, boy, where you going?" I screamed.

"Ain't no boy here, Mary," he replied.

"No sir, you are right. You ain't no boy at all, but *boy* where is the money you owe me?" We were standing toe-to-toe.

"I got money, but I ain't got no money for you, Mary."

"What? Why not?"

"Because I'm saving it to get me one of them new gals they got coming in from Helena later."

"You're saving it for what?"

"I am saving it to get me one of those gals."

"Saving the money? Is that what you say?" I looked off toward the Cascade Mountain Range.

"No problem."

I started to walk away. I stopped. I had gotten several paces away from the hired hand before I thought about what he said.

Then, I walked back to face him. Suddenly, and without warning, I unloaded a left-hand cross. The punch dropped him.

I stood over him for a moment to inspect the damage. It would do. I calmly returned to the bar, sat down, and finished my drink.

"What was that all about, Mary?" asked the bartender.

"What?"

"What! You just knocked out a man! He's still out cold on the street!"

"Oh, that. He refused to pay me what he owed me on his laundry bill. Now, look at him. His bill is paid in full."

A knockout blow to the head of a debtor was a form of charity in Montana in those days. The encounter could have been worse. The sheer enormity of my hands flopped over a rifle made it difficult to trigger the weapon at times, but it was quite an intimidating sight. A gunshot was far worse than a punch.

The Winchester's trigger guard was stylized. They began manufacturing the elegant Winchester rifles after the Civil War. Thank God they didn't have the Henrys or Winchesters, the repeating rifles, back then. There would have been far more casualties. There were already too many casualties.

When a debtor saw me coming, the oversized mitts, the mug of a man, the broad shoulders, the long arms hanging well past the cuffs of my sleeves, the height, the layers of baggy clothing, the history of knocking out ranchers with one punch, I am sure I looked like a very rough, and capable, man wearing a dress. The rifle, the cigars, the disposition, all played a role in how the town developed. Like it or not, folks had to figure out a way to respect me or else. This probably meant something about showing folks how their attitudes could change, given the right circumstances.

My behavior gave them the right circumstances, alright. I was the oddity that scared the Hell out of them. I absolutely shocked them out of bigotry, made them see that bigotry was wrong and could be overcome. I was the first to force the locals to respect the rights of a woman. The massive hands, the height, the weight, the vulgarity, the hard work, the cigars — it all meant something to the evolution of the Old West. It meant we could change. It meant we could accept women as full citizens.

I may have been the first, but if Cascade could do it for me, it could do it for everyone. Folks were fond of saying we were trailblazers, but we weren't just blazing trails. It was far bigger than that. We were blazing the entire country, every inch of it. And it was a mighty big country, too.

They started getting used to the idea. I was doing this and doing that, and just when folks settled into the notion that I was going to be treated fairly, bigotry aside, this poor excuse for a janitor, poor excuse for a white man, started to cause problems at the Mission. He, of all people, took offense at getting less money than a colored woman. I didn't have a problem with it. I had a problem with him.

I was his boss. I was skilled as a carpenter, mason, planter, and a host of other things. He was unskilled, and he was lazy, at that. I did twice the work of any man and three times the work of the janitor. You can say he had an entitled attitude to even dare suggest that he should receive the same pay as Mary Fields.

There was a rumor that he had complained to the bishop that no colored woman should be paid more than any white man, regardless of the circumstances. If he didn't get what was coming to him, there would be a problem at the Mission. I figured I could help him get what was coming to him, and it wasn't exactly what he had in mind. I was well aware that the janitor packed a pistol. Most folks did. So, the next battle I fought in Montana would not involve my fists. It would involve my .38.

Chapter Eleven

I built the Mission's chapel, steeple, schoolhouse, and dormitory. I built the stable stone by stone, the garden, and the hen house, and I built it all without much of a budget. I did it all for just nine dollars a week. It was an act of charity.

Of course, the skill of a carpenter, a mason, and a farmer were required. If you didn't possess those skills, if you couldn't do it yourself in the wilds of Montana, a tradesman wasn't likely to come bouncing along to do it for you.

I was also the Mission's groundskeeper. That meant the girls, the nuns, the priest, and our guests would have lawns across a beautiful campus to behold rather than an open field. It was hard work keeping the grounds from becoming overridden by weeds.

The land in Montana yearns to go back to original unbroken prairie, or the rowdy patches of nappy scrub brush that grows sporadically on mountainsides. Naturally, I cursed at the girls and the nuns and the bishop and whoever else trampled across the grounds when the grounds were freshly cut. I knew they were preoccupied with their faith, but I had to remind them in the best way I knew how.

I tended to the chickens and horses, grew vegetables, hitched the team to a wagon to go on supply runs or pick up a visitor in town, and more importantly, I packed a shotgun and .38 to keep ambitious bandits and Indians at bay. I did all of this for little or no pay.

The Mission allotted me the paltry sum of nine dollars a week, which was barely enough to keep me liquored up. I didn't complain. I lived at the Mission and ate the Mission's food, so I had to factor that into what I was paid. I managed to get by on homemade cigars. I always had work, so I didn't want for anything other than work clothes. The nuns once out-fitted me with a proper dress, but I was a sight to see in a proper dress. I felt more comfortable wearing work clothes and preferably the work clothes of a man. Anyway, all was well until the Mission decided to hire a white man to work under my supervision.

It seems that the only business the white man was good at was filing complaints with the bishop and the nuns. It was clear that he had designs on taking over my job as foreman at the Mission. The trouble was he was unskilled.

He couldn't do any carpentry, masonry, couldn't hitch a team, couldn't grow vegetables, and definitely couldn't scare away bandits or ambitious Indians. But he could definitely make it his business to complain to the nuns and the bishop whenever I got rowdy, cursed, knocked out a fellow, or got good and liquored up. He said no "nigger" should be in charge of "nothing" in Montana and colored folks should never receive better pay than a white man, according to his mind. He was trouble from the start.

The handy man was, at best, a helper. I was the boss. He ended up doing little more than leaning against a broom all day as the Mission's janitor. He packed a .45 and a bad temper. I packed a .38 and an even worse temper. The two were bound to clash, and when they did, I was more than ready.

The first secret to being good at drawing a pistol in Montana, and really anywhere, was to draw first, and that wasn't really such a big secret, either. That was the first rule in a place where typically there were no rules. And the second, and final, rule covered the importance of not only being first at the draw, but the added importance of being accurate. One without the other made for a predictably bad result.

Those two rules were all that mattered to me when it came to finally dealing with the janitor's bigotry and his .45. I heard rumors that the janitor's father was a Copperhead, having fought for the Confederacy during the Civil War. That made sense. His father must have raised him in a way that made him well versed in ignorance, because it took an awful lot of ignorance for him to believe he could take on the likes of me. The clash began on the very hour the janitor announced he was unwilling to take orders from a colored woman any longer.

"I want you to start cleaning the chimney flues after you finish sweeping the hallways," I said.

"You can want to be Chairman of the Territorial Legislative Assembly, but you need to win an election first," he replied, mysteriously.

"I am hitching the team and running to town. Make sure the flues is clean by the time I get back, hear?"

I knew the flues weren't going to be clean upon my return from town the instant the words left my mouth. The janitor had deceit on his mind. There was bound to be conflict and retaliation.

Chapter Twelve

I drove the team into town. I got supplies and headed back to the Mission. I didn't bother stopping at the saloon. I knew bandits were somewhere out on the prairie that day. I could feel it.

Of course, I was right.

Mexican bandits rode up out of the distance and pulled up their mounts alongside the wagon, bouncing around in their saddles like half-full sacks of potatoes. There were two of them.

They wore black hats with oversized, floppy brims, red bandanas, bright red and white checked shirts that looked like tablecloths, and angry-looking silver spurs. They had barrel chests and short legs dangling free of the irons, physiques that might have been perfect for climbing the Sierra Madre Oriental a few generations back, but less than perfect for robbing stagecoaches in Montana.

The Mexicans' horses were decked out in expensive, deep leather saddles. The saddle cloths were busy with the colors orange, blue, and yellow sewn into the fabric. When the Mexicans grinned, their pencil mustaches worked upward in the shadows cast over their faces by their sombreros. Of course, they showed the butts of .45's turned backward in the holsters on elaborate gun belts. The mere sight of the guns made most travelers as good as robbed, but that didn't pertain to me. As usual, I wasn't in the mood for foolishness.

I eyeballed the crew. I didn't halt my wagon. I didn't even ease the team. I didn't wish to concede anything that looked like fear, not during this incident, not ever. Fear is the bridesmaid of death on the prairie.

I figured the Mexicans probably spied only one figure seated on the buckboard of the wagon from a distance. This typically meant the wagon would be easy to rob. Usually, men rode in twos to discourage stick ups.

I don't know whether it was the size of my mitts flopped over the lock plate of the Winchester, the broad shoulders, the cigar smoke, the mean face, the black skin, the confident manner, or possibly all six, but the Mexicans eased their mounts, chatted briefly, turned their horses away, and rode off.

Truthfully, I was a little shaken by the bandits. I was good at not letting my true feelings show. The best gunfight is the one you bluff your way out of. When bullets start to fly, anything can happen. In a gunfight, there are winners and losers. Typically, there are no ties.

I turned up the flask of whiskey I sheltered under my coat. It was really good whiskey, too. It burned like a fire ball as it went down. It was the kind of burn that had no trouble getting your attention.

I was still a little jumpy from the brush with the Mexicans when I got back to the Mission. I was in no mood for foolishness. However, I figured that's exactly what the janitor had in store for me.

I gave him explicit instructions prior to leaving the Mission. If he hadn't cleaned the flues, as instructed, there would be trouble. I was the boss. I was perfectly ready, willing, and able to enforce my authority if he decided to test me. He was spoiling for a fight. I wasn't the type to run from a good fight.

Chapter Thirteen

Predictably, the work was not done. The flues were not clean. The floors were not swept. Furthermore, it didn't seem that the janitor was inclined to do any work at all. Instead, he merely leaned against a broom with a smirk on his face.

"Did I, or did I not, tell you to sweep the floors and clean the flues before I left for town?"

"You did, but that don't change nothing. I ain't gotta do shit for you, lady. I don't take orders from no colored woman, not in Montana, not anywhere, hear?"

We faced each other at the schoolhouse door. The girls and the nuns were engaged with their lessons in the classrooms. The bell was not due to ring for another fifteen minutes or so. There were no spectators. Nevertheless, the spectacle of a confrontation on school grounds was inevitable.

I was wearing enough clothing for two women, as usual. I wore men's trousers under my oversized dress. The wool overcoat I was wearing was buttoned up to the neck. I let my arms dangle at my sides, which meant my wrists and hands cleared the coat sleeves by a good inch or two. However, the coat made it difficult to move freely.

The janitor, on the other hand, was a wiry sort of fellow, precisely the type it was not wise to underestimate. He had a scar across the bridge of his nose, which suggested that he was accustomed to a scrape. He wore a plaid short. No vest. His arms swung freely along his thighs.

I knew the janitor's real name was Igor Bellanova, but he went by the alias, Jeff, in honor of Jefferson Davis, the Confederate president. Unlike Igor, Irina, his wife, had no trouble using her real name. The contrasts didn't end there.

While his wife was an elegant woman, Igor was quite the opposite. He was crude. Igor's father was crude, too.

Igor's father was a Copperhead. He went to his grave sore at Mr. Lincoln for what had been done to liberate the South. Igor's family was of Slavic descent, which meant his family tree ran across the sea to the Russian Empire of the 15th Century. The Slavic blood gave Igor a fiery temper and a ruddy complexion. It was well known in Cascade that Igor had already beaten a murder charge in open court. The folks in Cascade knew everything about Igor, except possibly his real name. This record, together with the .45, meant Igor was trouble.

Similarly, the folks of Cascade thought they knew me, too. The problem was there was a lot about me that was not knowable. For instance, I knew my family tree, like Igor's, ran across the sea. However, the difference was I didn't know exactly where it ended up. Like Igor, I had a fiery temper. Unlike Igor, I had a knockout punch to match my temper. If the knockout punch didn't work, I had the .38 to fall back on.

"You got a problem with me, partner?" I invited Jeff to place his manhood on display.

"I got no problem having a problem with you, *lady*. You got a problem with me having a problem with you?" He placed emphasis on the word lady, like he hated even the thought of it.

"Sounds like you're a little mixed up, Igor."

He looked at me sideways as though calling him by his real

name, Igor, instead of his alias, Jeff, meant that I was in on to some kind of secret.

If he actually had a reward out on his head somewhere, and he believed I found out about it, Jeff would have every reason to shoot me dead on the spot. Like the wolf attack, it was a simple matter of survival.

I looked deeply into his eyes, stared at them, really.

I didn't want to blink or show any fear by looking away. However, I clocked his every muscle in my peripheral vision. I looked for any warning he was about to draw. I had no choice.

"How so? I ain't mixed up at all," Igor said.

"Then, suppose you explain why you ain't done no work today."

"Ain't done no work today I am figuring because I don't see no cause to do no work around here just on a colored woman's say so."

"That so?"

"Yelp, that would be the nature of things."

Jeff knew I had the .38. I knew Jeff had the .45. The issue was joined.

"Igor, I tell you what I'm gonna do."

"Suppose you spare me your ideas on what you're gonna do or what work needs to be done around here, unless, of course, you figure out a way to become a white man to do the telling."

If there was going to be a draw anywhere in the Montana Territory, you didn't need to be just quick at the draw. That was not enough. You needed to be the quickest. That was a huge distinction. In my case, it wasn't only whether Jeff's hands moved or his muscles twitched that counted. The things that were in his head counted, too. Actually, everything mattered when it came to anticipating a draw, everything.

For example, I knew Igor hated women, and he definitely hated me, a colored woman. This would influence his judgment. Hatred would make his fingers itchy. Hatred was a weakness. It made Igor predictable.

I also knew Igor wanted to replace me as foreman at the Mission, even though he didn't have the skill to do so. He felt entitled to more pay than a colored woman, even though he did less work. This, too, made him more likely to draw.

Igor knew I didn't care about his hatred for women or anything else that bugged him. I was going to insist on respect. He knew that if he decided to box or wrestle me, I would make short work of him, dismiss the myth of male superiority, and promptly break his nose or worse. This left gunplay as his only option.

Then, there was the issue of the alias and reward posters out on him that were probably tacked up somewhere in the Pacific Northwest. If calling him out by his real name bothered him, it was probably for good reason. If he was a wanted man, he would be very anxious to draw.

Finally, Igor believed I always packed my .38 beneath my apron. He figured the coat would make it difficult for me to draw quickly. He was wrong. I didn't always pack the .38 under my apron. That routine would have made me predictable. I was tactical, not predictable. Therefore, I often changed my patterns. The .38 was in the pocket of my coat that day, not under my apron.

Shockingly, Igor began raising his voice: "I tell you…"

I drew. I didn't trigger the .38, but I drew. I was first. Igor drew, too, but late.

I was staring down Igor's .45. He was staring down the .38. Nobody moved. No shots were fired—not yet, anyway.

The bell rang. The nuns and the girls came pouring out of the classrooms. They witnessed the spectacle.

"Put those guns away!" Sister Amadeus screamed, rushing out of a classroom in horror. She placed emphasis on the word "guns," like the word itself was an evil created in the lowest, most faraway places in Hell and the Catholic God had told her so.

She stepped between that evil, showing precisely the same fervor and courage she once displayed to stop hostilities between the Blackfeet and Flatheads. Back then, she was new to the prairie, and she still hadn't learned to speak a single word of Crow, but the tribes had already learned to trust the spirit of the "Black Gown," as she was called. The sides were painted, showed feathers, and the arrows had already started to fly. However, the sight of the "Black Gown" stopped the bloodshed. Similarly, she showed courage stepping between the .45 and the .38.

The nuns shepherded the girls back into the classrooms, trying to shield their eyes from the spectacle. No shots were fired. It didn't matter. The girls, the nuns, literally everyone, had seen the exchange. We put our guns away without further incident.

Just as a nation cannot un-live its history, and once rung, a bell cannot be un-rung, I could not take back the standoff. I didn't want to take it back, either. I actually enjoyed pointing the .38 at Jeff. It still felt good, and in his case, I am not sure I wouldn't do it again, if given a second chance.

Chapter Fourteen

The bishop got the news the next day. The story he heard was inconsistent with the facts. He was told that I had drawn my .38 and held the janitor at gunpoint. Nothing else.

The bishop acted impulsively. Instead of holding a hearing, he fired me without learning any of the facts and circumstances.

Nevertheless, I insisted on a hearing, on the ability to defend myself, and save my job. I pled with the bishop to call witnesses. I assured him not a single eye-witness would come forward to substantiate the claim that I had acted inappropriately. Sure, the incident should not have happened on Mission grounds. I would concede that point. However, I would never concede the point that I did not have the right to defend myself.

More to the point, I would never concede the point that I was less than Igor, or anyone else, simply because Igor was a white man. Instead, I would appeal to reason. If witnesses were called at a hearing, I argued, the facts would speak for themselves. They wouldn't support the conclusion that I was wrong. If it came down to a case of my word against Igor's, I was sure I would be able to shake Igor's story through the wonders of cross examination, if indeed he lied about me being the aggressor.

The bishop didn't bother with reason. He already had his

mind made up about me, the liquor, the cursing, the fighting, the cigar smoking, the men's clothing, and now this, the threat of gunplay on Mission grounds. I was finished.

Sister Amadeus, the Mother Superior of the Mission, was powerless to reverse his decision. She was outranked by the bishop. My days at the Mission had come to an abrupt, and unceremonious, end.

Chapter Fifteen

Cascade, Montana, May 1913

The thought of a termination—my own—cut into the daydream. It brought me back to the here and now. That's when I saw the reporter's face again. He had listened to the whole story. There were tears in his eyes. He didn't offer words of encouragement. He didn't offer solace. He didn't talk to me of the endless justice of an evolving nation. He didn't talk at all. He just sat there, stunned.

I heard the telegraph spitting out news across the cable from all around the globe. The nation was catching up to the idea of justice, finally. Mr. Lincoln had done his part. There was a tomb in Springfield, Illinois that proved the point.

I wasn't wearing men's clothing. I was wearing trousers under a full-length grey dress with white lace collar. The collar looked similar to the crocheted lace doilies that were popular in fine households. I dreamed of seeing a fine household again, like the Dunne household I left behind in Toledo.

I was nervous. I didn't know what to say or even what to do with my hands. The reporter had stopped asking questions. He was staring off toward the horizon, and the horizon wasn't even in view from the news room. I felt worse for the reporter than I did for myself.

I could control my feelings. I was born a slave. I knew injustice firsthand. However, I never would have guessed that the triumph over injustice that I enjoyed in Cascade would be cut short by bad luck and a poor decision by the Catholic Church.

I looked good in grey, and I wore the lace collar proudly. White is the color of the clouds. I realized the getup didn't make me look beautiful, but at least I wasn't wearing men's clothing and a bowler on top of a wool hat. Furthermore, I didn't bother bringing a Winchester to the interview. That was quite an improvement. I still packed the .38, but I was probably getting a little soft in my old age.

I wondered how many souls would attend the ceremony to hang my portrait in Cascade. The Montana Express settled the wilderness of Montana all the way to the Pacific, populating Great Falls and Butte along the way. That railroad had helped transform this part of the world into a mighty empire. I wondered if the railroad would bring a crowd to witness the portrait hanging today, my final hoorah. I hoped our history would not be lost. Instead, I hoped the memory of what we accomplished here would last forever.

That's why I spoke to the reporter, and that's why I hoped the portrait hanging would draw a crowd. I wanted everyone to see the portrait of "Stagecoach" Mary Fields, pioneer.

I wanted everyone to know that at the end of the day I had succeeded in capturing the respect of the folks of Cascade.

The mayor hadn't managed to arrive yet. He was many hours behind schedule. I knew the protocol of what happened when folks finally decided to honor you. There was always lateness and complications and disorganization—chaos, really. I had seen it happen so often to others that I knew it by heart. I had played it over and over in my mind across days and weeks leading up to the ceremony.

But I remained calm and wanted to talk to the reporter

about the old days, and we started talking again. He asked me what happened after the bishop fired me. That got things going.

I told him that Sister Amadeus, the Mother Superior of the Mission, a woman intensely faithful to the teachings of the Risen Christ, recognized the bishop was wrong. She made it her business to right the wrong in a clever way.

A couple of reporters joined in, surrounding me to hang on my every word. They asked for my autograph. I guessed my autograph was worth something. So, I obliged. I signed a few newspapers.

One of the reporters passed me a flask of whiskey. That got things going in earnest from that point on, joking and walking and sitting down and standing back up again and walking around. The reporters laughed each time I threw up the flask and took a belt. You could almost forget I was even capable of drawing a .38 in a schoolhouse at that moment.

I told the reporter about Sister Amadeus's plan. She didn't have the power to overrule a bishop. That was against Church protocol. However, she had the wherewithal to work around Church policy.

She didn't have the authority to pay my salary or restore me to my rightful job as foreman, but she could give me money to buy a restaurant. If I opened a restaurant, I could feed the folks of Cascade and make money doing it. This was a perfect plan. With Sister Amadeus's artful thought process, I was on to the next stage of my life, the stage when I ventured out on my own as a business woman.

Chapter Sixteen

Montana Territory, January 1893

If Sister Amadeus's plan to slip me the money to start a restaurant was perfect in theory, it quickly proved to be a disaster in practice. The reason was simple. While I might have been good with a .38, I was terrible at business.

I didn't have the heart to turn down folks who were hungry, even if they were broke. It was Cascade. It was Montana. It was before the railroad succeeded in turning many of the towns in the Pacific Northwest into boom towns. It seemed like nearly every ranch hand, copper miner, farmer, and drunken cowboy who passed the restaurant was hungry and broke. This meant I was destined to be hungry and broke, too.

The restaurant, like Cascade itself, admittedly wasn't much to look at. It wasn't fancy. It was an unpainted clapboard house with a tin roof and a narrow boardwalk in front that kept folks from walking through the mud when it rained. No hand painted sign. The rain and harsh winters had their way with the clapboards long before I bought the place. The good thing about the restaurant is it was close to the saloon in town, and the bad thing about the restaurant is it was close to the saloon in town.

In the saloon, I swiftly acquired the reputation as a cook who couldn't refuse a customer, even when the customer had no money. I cooked. I stocked the restaurant with plenty of food and supplies. I was rapidly running out of both. This sent me to the saloon where I was allowed to drink whiskey for free. This only made matters worse. A saloon, whiskey, and a business failure weren't part of a formula for success.

"Mary, why in the devil don't you make your customers pay before you serve them?" the bartender at the local saloon asked, looking up from his work. He had just set me up with a shot of whiskey on the house. The saloon was empty. The ranch hands still hadn't come in from the prairie.

"Why in the devil don't you mind your own business?"

"Mary, I am not trying to tell you what to do. I am just trying to look out for you."

"I know the advice comes from a good place, but I have my ways."

"You could take your restaurant to Helena or Great Falls or Butte and make a fortune, but you have it in Cascade. There ain't no fortune to be had here in little Cascade. We are poor folk in the middle of nowhere out here."

"Nobody tells me what to do. Nobody tells me where to go. These is my folks out here, and if they are hungry, and I got the food to feed them, they are going to get fed."

"That's fine, Mary. You have a big heart. You've proven that. Everybody loves you for that..."

"Everybody, that is, except the bishop of the Montana diocese," I said.

"Okay, you got a point there, but do you see there is a problem with what you're saying?"

"What's the problem?"

"It is called arithmetic. If you spend more than you earn, you eventually go broke."

Unlike the Montana Territory as a whole, I didn't evolve any after the conversation with the bartender. I couldn't.

Cascade had accepted me, a former slave, as a full citizen exactly as I was.

I was invited to drink whiskey in her saloons, babysit her children, and feed her hungry. She forgave me when I got into gunfights. If I argued with a paying customer in the saloon, she didn't take offense. If she got word that I had behaved poorly or cursed out a Catholic nun, she took it in stride. She didn't condemn me. She never criticized me for wearing men's clothing or scandalized my name for not taking a man's hand in marriage. If I knocked out a ranch hand or a copper miner along the way, she didn't think anything of it. That's why, if I eventually went broke feeding her hungry ranch hands, farmers, copper miners, and cowboys, I would just have to accept that outcome as my destiny.

I didn't give in to failure. Sure, I kept feeding everyone who asked for help. I gave the local children candy whenever they came calling, and they came calling often. I did laundry and babysat and did practically any odd job I could get to save the restaurant. It didn't work. The restaurant closed. I was broke.

I was already sixty years old at the time, and broke. I had nowhere to turn, and the Montana Territory is brutally cold in winter, and oppressively hot in summer, especially when you have nowhere to turn.

I couldn't return to the Mission. The bishop had made sure of that. I really didn't have anywhere to turn.

Some folks acquire bad luck at birth. I was one of them. I was no stranger to bad luck or hard times. I had suffered more than my share of both back on the plantation in Tennessee.

It wasn't only the audacity to say and do whatever I pleased in Cascade that made me a pioneer of the Old West. It wasn't only the insistence that folks respect my rights. It was also the courage to survive bad luck, to persevere the adversity of slavery, poverty, challenging terrain, cruel summers and harsh winters, and the sting of bigotry, to overcome the growing pains of the Pacific Northwest, even as black codes sponsored by Copperheads and others terrorized colored folks. Looking back, given what I had seen in life, the ignominy of a failed business scarcely mattered.

Still, I had no way out of my troubles, and the bitter cold of winter in Montana was unforgiving. If I figured out how to avoid freezing to death, I'd have a fairly good chance to see spring, for death frequently visited Montana. Sure, the locals didn't turn their backs on me in my time of need.

They offered me food, lodging at the local hotel, and free whiskey at the saloon. However, I needed much more. Charity aside, something historic was on the way. I needed a miracle. Soon, I would get one.

Chapter Seventeen

The miracle came in the form of a wanted poster. The posters were tacked up everywhere. The wind that blows through the Cascades, the same wind that has the reputation for disrespecting the cluster of weather-beaten clapboard buildings along the town's dusky main street, was the wind that sent the posters flapping.

The wanted posters were actually United States Postal Service announcements. Those announcements gave all comers the opportunity to bid on a contract to deliver mail. The route covered by the contract was known as the Star Route, a stage run from Cascade to railroad stations located in Helena, Great Falls, Billings, Butte, and Miles City. Those stations were where the mail drops were located. The successful bidder would be asked to meet the mail train, pick up the mail, secure the bundles on a stagecoach, and safely return the bundles to Cascade, and to do so faithfully, on time, and in the regular course of business.

The proposition sounded a lot better on paper than it was in reality. In reality, the work proposed was nearly impossible to perform, to perform on time, or at all. The reason is the route was across the unbroken wilds of Montana, and the unbroken wilds of Montana were no ordinary wilds.

The wilds of Montana included dangerous, nearly impassable terrain across rocky breaks and crevices, razor-sharp mountain ridges and passes, and the like. If this was not enough, the stagecoach would face the additional challenge of ambitious, and armed, bandits, hungry winter wolves, tribal warriors looking to exact revenge against interlopers, sub-zero temperatures, blizzards, and drifting snow. Nevertheless, young men, and only young men, lined up to apply for the job. For the men, the Star Route represented steady pay and a way out of their troubles. For the folks of Cascade, the Star Route represented a tenuous link to the civilized world. I didn't see any connection whatsoever between me and that link.

First, it was 1895. There had only been one woman in history who had won a contract to deliver mail on a stagecoach run, and she wasn't a colored woman. Second, I was over sixty years old at the time. The competitors for the job would be young men half my age. Third, the run was onerous. It was a job for two men, not a single colored woman.

The reason was the silhouettes of two figures atop the stagecoach, including a driver, who was also called a Charlie, brother whip, or simply a whip, and a shotgun messenger, who was called a problem, served as a deterrent to stagecoach robbers. The shotgun messenger sat alongside the driver with a shotgun in plain view to announce bad intentions to whoever dared to interfere with the run. In this respect, the shotgun messenger was the key ingredient.

Conversely, the silhouette of only one figure, even if the figure was a colored woman with a reputation for being tougher than any two men, wasn't likely to have quite the same effect.

Fourth, I didn't even own a stagecoach, so how on earth was I going to run a stagecoach to deliver mail or do anything else, really? Finally, I didn't own a team of six horses. The only beast I owned on four legs was a mule named Moses, and Moses wasn't likely to pull even one wheel of a stagecoach, no less the entire load. This logic seemed impeccable. Sister Amadeus thought otherwise.

Sister Amadeus saw the Star Route as a way out of my troubles. She believed in miracles. Why else would she think to go the Godforsaken corners of the territories to spread the Gospel? In this spirit, she believed I could become the first colored woman in history to own a United States Postal Service contract to deliver mail on a stage run. Sister Amadeus was ambitious, but she wasn't unwise. She possessed direct evidence that I was up to the task of running an overland stagecoach. She had seen me in action. She had seen me perform miracles. She had faith.

However, in Montana, and probably everywhere else, there is more to a miracle than faith. In this case, a miracle would also require a team of six horses and a stagecoach. I had neither. You could have all the faith in the world, and you weren't likely to run a stagecoach without the stagecoach, now were you? Sister Amadeus had the answer to this riddle as well, and the answer didn't involve prayer.

Unknown to the Catholic Church, Sister Amadeus had the facility to loan me six horses to form a team and the stagecoach, which would leave only one remaining obstacle. I would have to earn the contract by winning a contest.

The United States Postal Service organized a competition to see which bidder could hitch a team of six horses the fastest. The fastest man, or woman, would win the contract. This seemed fair.

The stage was set. The nuns, ranchers, farm hands, bartenders, and literally everyone around town, except the bishop, crowded along the street to watch the competition.

The leather straps, brass chains and rings, yokes, lines, and the rest of the equipment forming the harnesses were tangled and piled in the dust. The horses were waiting. The other competitors, ranch hands, farmers, livery hands, and copper miners, all stood at the ready. The first to hitch a team to a stagecoach would win the contract.

The postal inspector judging the contest held a red handkerchief aloft. We all waited for the signal. The second the red handkerchief dropped to the ground, the race was on. All eyes were on that handkerchief.

Chapter Eighteen

The red handkerchief fell. The race was on!

A roar went up in the crowd of onlookers that matched the intensity of a theatre full of spectators witnessing boxers trade punches at the center of the ring in the last round of a prize fight. There was cursing, whistling, and taunting. The spectators didn't seem to mind that the Ursuline nuns, the women of God, were present to hear the noise. The nuns didn't seem to mind, either.

The nuns screamed lustily. They jumped and swung their fists through the air. The wind caught the hem of their garments and filled their black habits, like sails. They didn't care. They wanted me to win.

"Are you Ursulines? Yes, you are! Are you Ursulines? Yes, you are!" the nuns chanted, waving their fists.

The rest of the spectators chanted, too. The crowd screamed, pleaded with the competitors, urged the competitors they backed to go faster, as if urging could help a single contestant solve the riddle of the harnesses.

I had hitched many teams. I knew how to solve the riddle. I knew the pleas from the audience would not affect the outcome. I didn't need a miracle. I knew I was faster than any of the men, and I was faster by a lot.

While the men sprinted, I walked confidently, smoking away at a homemade cigar. The straps, chains, collars of the harnesses remained on the ground in impossibly complex piles. The key was to know how to untangle the mess, quickly. In order to do so, you really had to know your stuff.

I calmly lifted the leather straps and brass chains, analyzed the mess, and began solving the riddle. The other men thrashed away, pulling the straps, dropping the chains, and generally succeeding at making the complex tangle of equipment into even bigger messes. Some of the men cursed. Others stopped to collect their thoughts. Still others consulted members of the audience for tips on what to do to solve the riddle. None of it worked. I was in the lead.

I segregated my equipment into clean rows, leather straps in one row, chains in another, yokes, hames, and the rest of the harness in the proper order. I was already ready to hitch the team. I walked the first pair of horses back to the equipment. The horses stood proudly erect, ears twitching, necks bowed, fully compliant. The triumphant process of hitching the first pair of horses of my team was already underway.

The nuns cheered.

Meanwhile, only one of the young men had brought his harness even close to order. The others were making little, if any, progress.

"Two back, two back, two back now," I whispered to the horses.

It was a special code between horse woman and horse. The team understood the code quite well. It was a mysterious language. The nuns had heard it before on Mission grounds. The rest of the crowd, and probably the other contestants as well, didn't have the foggiest idea of what the code meant. They had as much hope of breaking the code as they had of solving the riddle of the harnesses.

The harnesses, including brass hames, spider, hip drops, breachings, turnbacks, tug chains, quarter straps, girth bands, belly bands, butt straps, bottom hames straps, and bridles, including bits, tongue chains, reins, and blinders, were organized and thrown over the backs of the beasts, and cinched, and then I backed the team into position to hitch the whole affair to the shaft of the coach.

I had hitched the remaining four horses, side by side, six horses in all standing in two horse pairs. All of the near side horses, the horses standing on the left side of the pairs, and the off's, the horses standing on the right side of the pairs, stood motionless, peaking out of the slits in their blinkers.

My stagecoach was ready to roll. I had won, and won easily. I sat triumphantly on the box. I blew a kiss up to the sky over Montana that is high and deep and all around. I had won!

A cheer went up from the nuns. In a way, they had won, too.

Several competitors threw their hats down in disgust. Others looked at their feet as they shuffled off and disappeared in the crowd. Still others talked excitedly to their backers, searching for an excuse, any excuse, to explain how they had lost the contest to a woman.

Mysteriously, I had disappeared. When the nuns rushed up to the stagecoach to congratulate me, they couldn't solve the mystery of my disappearance any more than my competitors could solve the riddle of the harnesses. I was gone, and they didn't have a clue about where to look to find me.

The only person who had any idea where to find me was Sister Amadeus. She marched off to the local saloon. There, she found me seated at the bar.

Mother Superior didn't upset the Risen Christ, or soil her spirit, by entering the saloon. She didn't need to set foot in the saloon. She could see me through the bat wing doors. The trail of cigar smoke in the street had led her to the spot.

I had already thrown back my first shot of whiskey. I

slammed the empty glass on the bar. That was my signal to the bartender to pour more whiskey. Sister Amadeus didn't intervene. She simply left me alone to celebrate.

Shortly after that day, the paperwork was completed, and I was awarded a contract by the United States Postal Service to become a Star Route carrier. This made me the first colored woman in American history to be so honored. I was indeed something of a pioneer.

I performed my duties with distinction. I was never late to meet the mail delivery at the railroad stations, even when I had to wear snow shoes to hitch the team. I never lost a day to illness, even when the temperatures were sub-zero, the wind was cruel, and the winters were long. I protected the mail against attacks by thieves and bandits.

The evolution of the region depended on mail delivery. It was our only link to the civilized world. The mail contained news, letters, money, and other items. I protected those precious items for nearly eight years of my life. I carried a shotgun and pistol to get the job done.

If weapons didn't discourage those looking to make a fortune by subverting the mail deliveries, I was known to stand up on the box to show the full extent of my six-foot frame. I was more than enough woman to get the job done. I was more than enough woman to intimidate. By doing so, a woman who was born a slave in Hickman County, Tennessee, a woman who appreciated that Mr. Lincoln had brought the Civil War to the doorstep of the South, a very black woman who sometimes wore men's clothing, often cursed and smoked cigars, and always welcomed a fist fight and a stiff drink, had finally become financially independent. I was finally able to donate to charitable causes. I was finally free.

Chapter Nineteen

I exercised my newly found financial independence to do-nate generously to the one thing I loved unconditionally, the game of baseball.

Cascade fielded a baseball team of exactly nine players. No substitutes. We dressed our nine players in baggy wool uni-forms adorned with a fancy letter "C" embroidered across the chest. We were called the Cascade Kings.

The players bloused their trousers at the knee, exposing high white stockings. Their white caps matched the stockings. The bills of their caps were grey, and every player possessed his own leather mitt, which was an oddity at the time. In those days, the fingers of the mitts were splayed, untethered. There was no webbing between the fingers.

We suffered great expense to outfit our team with genuine *Louisville Slugger* bats, white ash tooled on a lathe in an actual woodworking shop. The manufactured bats were weighed, measured, and balanced to specification, and the *John Hillerich* label was proudly burned into the wood. At the time, other town teams still sported an odd assortment of handmade bats. We paid handsomely to use the same bats as professional teams.

I loved watching our boys confidently loosen up prior to the start of games. They played catch along the sidelines. The sounds of the game of baseball were intoxicating, the sound the ball makes when it pops the pocket of the mitt, the chatter between players, the crack of the bat during batting practice. I also loved watching the arc of fly balls to the deepest parts of the outfield, especially on cloudless days.

The Cascade Kings took on all comers. We even barnstormed across the Pacific Northwest looking for competition. We were that good. In fact, I argued we were on par with more than a few major league teams.

Whenever "Steamboat" Billy Wall was on the mound, our team was nearly invincible. If a major leaguer could hit Billy, I'd have to see it with my own eyes to believe it. He was that good.

Billy was at least a head taller than the other players. His eyes were the color of the sky, and he had a mop of strawberry blonde hair he controlled by repeatedly taking off his cap, rubbing the sweat off his brow with the sleeve of his uniform, combing back his flowing hair, and fitting his cap over the back of his head again. He had the fluid, poetic movements of a born athlete.

There was music in even his ordinary movements, like simply walking off the field, working his fingers into a mitt, or sitting on the bench with his legs crossed. All eyes were on Billy. Above all else, he wasn't merely handsome. He was a heart throb, a natural, a cinch as leading man for any photographer. Billy had it all.

However, the best part of Billy, the part that made him the talk of baseball, was the way he pitched the ball. He could really hum it. He threw it so fast you could hear it hissing as it cut the air on its way to home plate. The batters he faced out in Montana couldn't catch up to his fast ball no matter how hard they tried, because his fastball didn't cut the air flat. Instead, it danced around in the air before it popped the catcher's mitt.

Nobody could hit that pitch. Nobody. The opposing players made themselves look silly trying to make contact. Actually, it was hard to even find a catcher who could catch it.

When the batters got wise and started looking for the fast
ball, Billy would fool them by throwing his knuckle curveball.
You could actually hear that pitch change speeds in midair before it reached home plate. It was comical watching batter after batter swing so hard, and so futilely, that they often lost
their caps in the process. Imagine the ignominy of stooping to
pick up your cap out of the dust after Billy struck you out.

Billy threw strike after strike and pitched no hitter after no
hitter. That boy could really throw. He was a legend.

Now, if nobody could hit Billy's fast ball, how could anyone score a run to beat Cascade? It didn't matter what color
uniform the opposition wore while they were sent out of the
batter's box cursing. It could have been the red stockings of
the Boston Red Sox, the blue jerseys of Cleveland, the white
stockings of Chicago, or even the red interlocking "N" and
"Y" of the New York Cubans. It didn't matter. Nobody hit
Billy. Nobody.

I didn't coach the team, but I felt that I could have coached
the team. I posed for all team photographs wearing my finest
pressed dresses. I arrogantly smoked a cigar and didn't bother
taking it out of my mouth for the photographer, like I was the
team owner.

The Cascade side was unquestionably sharp, strictly major
league grade. I argued with anyone who would listen that
Cascade, assuming Billy was pitching, was better than half the
teams in the major leagues. I dreamed of the day we could take
on a major league team and prove the point. Then, one day I
got my wish.

The Louisville Colonels of the National League were in town. They were at the bottom of the standings that year, but they were still technically a major league team. When they agreed to play us, they had no way of knowing if we were up to par. Of course, we planned to pitch Billy against them. The Louisville Colonels didn't know what was about to hit them.

The Colonels looked magnificent in their wonderfully tailored flannel uniforms. They spread out across the outfield grass during pre-game warmups, like a mirage. The uniforms were of the highest-quality flannel. It was the kind of fabric you'd expect to see in the finest men's three-piece suits sold in New York, Philadelphia, or Boston, the kind of suits you see featured in newspaper advertisements for elegant young men able to pay a handsome price. The uniforms were probably made by a famous designer in a tailor's shop. The heavy wool of our baggy outfits was completely outclassed.

The major league uniforms featured a red shirt collar, red bow tie, a wide red belt, high red stockings, and an embroidered red team insignia over the breast pocket. Their shoes were made of soft leather, thin leather soles, and sharp silver cleats. The shoes looked more like elegant, polished dress shoes than anything you'd expect to see on a baseball diamond. The players hats were grey with flaming red bills. The players not wearing hats showed finely trimmed mustaches and fresh haircuts.

The Colonels looked good. They weren't merely a baseball team. They were an entire baseball operation. The arrogance of major leaguers showed in their very manner.

The Colonels spread out across the outfield during pregame warmups and effortlessly caught towering batting practice fly balls. Some of the fly balls hit our rickety clapboard outfield fence with a hollow thud. The outfield fence stood a distance of a little over three hundred fifty feet away from home plate.

I knew every inch of that fence. I raised the money from our local businessmen to build it. The clapboards were slopped with green paint. There were colorful signs painted on parts of the fence advertising the Cascade Courier, the Silver Dollar Saloon, and other local businesses.

On the infield, the Colonels executed their practice drills seamlessly, fielding ground balls smoothly, wheeling, and throwing the balls with purpose and accuracy to first base. The first baseman expertly caught each throw, turned, and fired the ball back to home plate. Louisville's warmup drills were a thing of beauty.

After the drills had reached a conclusion, Louisville surrendered the field to the home team. None of the Colonels bothered to even wonder if any of our local players showed talent. Instead, they talked confidently among themselves on the third baseline without bothering to acknowledge that they even had competition. They momentarily lost sight of the truth that all teams are inherently equal—at least, until the first pitch is thrown. However, Louisville's overconfident demeanor vanished the instant it was Billy's turn to take the mound.

Billy cut loose several warmup pitches. The ball popping the mitt was so loud it seemed like the report of gunfire. This caught the attention of everyone on Louisville's side of the field. Now, with the audience spellbound, Billy teased its sense of intrigue by ceasing to throw, breaking his routine, turning his back on home plate while walking over the rubber on the top of the mound, tipping his cap, holding the ball in his meat hand, and working a very long time at digging a hole near the rubber with his cleats.

It seemed as though Billy wanted it to be a perfect hole, so he spent plenty of time digging away. After he was satisfied, he brushed the top of the rubber with his cleats, tipped his cap yet again, signaled to the catcher that he was ready to throw more warmup pitches, leaned forward, sighted the target, and cut loose his legendary fast ball.

Now that he was loose, Billy tipped his cap and strode off the mound. He stood on the infield grass. The Colonels went on about their business at the bench, hefting bats, tossing aside gloves, searching for balls. Their confident demeanor had been restored. This lasted ever so briefly, until Billy began to throw again.

The sound of the ball hissing through the air on the way to popping the catcher's mitt caught their attention yet again. They gawked. That's when the confidence seemed to melt away. The Colonels began to whisper to each other and steal looks at Billy's fluid, effortless windup.

I walked behind home plate to get a better look. Billy was throwing magnificently. His fast ball hopped before it got to home plate. The breaking ball changed speed in midair and looked like it dropped off the edge of a table. These pitches looked unhittable. The sound of the fast ball popping the catcher's mitt needed no interpretation.

I walked across the field to the third baseline side of home plate. There, I met a gentleman wearing an expensive suit. There was a fake yellow carnation stuck in his left lapel button. He must have been a scout, an agent, a sportswriter, one of the team managers, or something important. He wore a straw boater with a hat band that matched Louisville's team colors.

"Don't worry, boys!" the gentleman said just loud enough to be heard over the pop of the catcher's mitt. "I've seen this type of boy before. Morning glory! Looks good warming up, but can't get anybody out in the hillbilly league. That's why he's here."

"What's that mean, mister?" I asked.

"What's what mean?"

"You called him a morning glory."

"Oh, that. That means he's a rummy, a loser, a flashy sort who looks fabulous in warmups, but can't pitch a lick in the game, not to the likes of the Colonels, anyway. They're big leaguers."

"You calling us hillbillies?"

"Why yes, madam, I believe I am. That's a fact. The way I see it—"

I dropped the gentleman with two swift punches.

I didn't bother to spit the cigar out of my mouth while doing so. There was no use in ruining a perfectly good cigar. The punches that did the job were thrown in combination, an uppercut followed by an overhand right.

As the punches landed, the gentleman's straw hat with the fancy silk hat band popped off his head. He made the mistake of misunderstanding that a challenge to our brand of baseball was more than a challenge involving only the game of baseball. It was a challenge to who we were as a people. It was a challenge to whether we were worthy to dream of progress with the rest of the nation. It was a suggestion that we were somehow inferior and rightfully excluded from the promise of an evolving nation. For the folks of Cascade, baseball wasn't only a game, but a plot played out across nine innings. In this way, the gentleman's challenge cut far too close to our character to ignore.

The gentleman nervously tried to collect his wits and struggle to his feet, but instead sort of clawed at my legs to help orient himself. He felt his mouth for blood. There was no blood. There was only ignominy.

I enjoyed the pleasure of hitting him with two punches, one for Cascade and one for me. I suppose the gentleman was lucky I didn't decide to hit him with a third and fourth punch, one for Montana and the fourth for the entire Pacific Northwest.

"Hey, you okay over there partner?" one of the Colonels yelled from the third baseline.

"Slip. It was just a slip," the gentleman said, picking up his straw hat and rising to his feet. "I am fine, just fine."

"Why're you touching your mouth then?" The player's question wasn't answered.

The gentleman's eyes were wide open. He looked me up and down, all six feet and two hundred pounds of me. He appeared unwilling to admit that he had been knocked down by a woman. So, he nervously walked away, looking over his shoulder as if to convince himself that what happened was not real.

Everybody else on the grounds, including the players, coaches, and the spectators, was mesmerized by Billy's warmup pitches. So, nobody saw the punch. They only saw the aftermath of the punch. Therefore, the gentleman's pride was intact.

I wondered how long Louisville's pride would remain intact. How many innings would it take for Louisville to lose its arrogance? I knew the chances were slim that a local team would have any success at all against a National League team. It didn't matter. I was free to dream.

Tony Mullane, on loan to Louisville from the Baltimore Orioles, was named the starting pitcher for Louisville.

Mullane was an Irishman who liked to drink hard apple

cider, curse, and throw spit balls. He was in the process of attempting to make a comeback to the big leagues following an early, and ill-advised, retirement. The Louisville manager thought it would be smart to test Mullane's arm against Cascade before signing his contract and allowing him to join the team. He wanted to see if Mullane still had his good stuff.

The rumor was that Mullane had once thrown a no-hitter in a major league game, but nobody could find statistics to confirm the rumor. There was much intrigue surrounding Mullane, including whispers that he could pitch with either hand, a rarity. If this was true, it probably meant he had perfected the art of throwing spit balls with either hand.

The coaches exchanged lineup cards at home plate. The umpire inspected the cards, took his time satisfying himself that everything was in order, and proceeded to roll the ball to the mound to signal the start of the game. The ball was a regulation ball, precisely the same ball umpires put into play in the majors. The battle was joined.

The crowd had swollen to dramatic proportion. It seemed that not a single soul from town was missing. There were ranch hands wearing chaps and leather vests, copper miners with lanterns and hard hats at their feet, women wearing dresses that swept the ground, nuns in black habits, and school children set free from school.

Cascade, the home team, was the first to take the field. This left behind the embarrassment of an empty bench, since Cascade, a town in the middle of nowhere that only recently had been incorporated, had the wherewithal to attract only nine players to their roster. Conversely, the mighty Colonels had the full roster of a major league ball club. The Louisville bench was crowded with players who were busy hefting bats, oiling mitts, reclining, standing up, walking around, spitting tobacco juice at the ground, chatting, and so on.

In the top of the first, Billy set down the Colonels in order. The batters never took the bats off their shoulders. They were looking to see what Billy had to offer, and he had plenty to offer, indeed.

The pitches hissed at the air before popping the catcher's mitt. The crowd of locals applauded politely. The suspicion was that Louisville had been instructed by their clever manager to not actually swing at any of Billy's pitches, but to report to the players waiting on deck about the speed and accuracy of his pitches. They were looking for signs that Billy had a flaw in his delivery that would serve to tip batters that his breaking ball was coming. These signs were called tells. Thus far, Billy's pitches were flawless. Furthermore, there were no tells in his delivery to give the Colonels an advantage.

Our side went down in order in the bottom of the first inning, as expected. Neither side had as much as fouled off a pitch. However, it really didn't look like a classic pitcher's duel. The reason is Cascade really didn't have any hitters in the lineup likely to pose any threat whatsoever to a big league pitcher like Mullane, and Mullane was indeed a big leaguer, regardless of which hand he decided to use to pitch. On the other hand, Louisville was stacked with power hitters, including their invincible cleanup hitter, the powerful Ducky Holmes.

I watched Billy's face as he glared over the top of his glove at the catcher's signals. He was using all of his energy to keep his pitch count low, but through the middle innings he had already begun to tire. This may have been due to the unusual way he warmed up that day. He took a series of warmup pitches. Then, he broke his normal routine by cooling off only to warm up yet again, sensing that the Colonels might have been scouting him. The second set of warmup pitches may have contributed to his lack of stamina, and Cascade would need plenty of stamina from Billy that day to avoid embarrassment.

This was a pitcher's duel in the sense that we were still hitless through six innings, but it wasn't a classic pitcher's duel. Mullane faced Cascade batters that had no prayer of making any contact whatsoever with major league pitching, and Mullane knew it. Conversely, Billy was throwing at dangerous hitter after dangerous hitter. He had to unleash his best stuff over and over, and he couldn't afford to yield a single hit. If Louisville scored even a single run, the game would be over.

However, the game wasn't over. In the top of the seventh, Billy began to rely on his knuckle curveball. That pitch began to fool the Colonels. He faced the middle of the lineup.

In the top of the seventh, Billy ran up the count to three balls and two strikes on the leadoff hitter. If the next pitch was a ball, the Colonels would have their first base runner of the game, their first sign of life. Cascade couldn't afford to concede even one run, and we definitely could not afford to let the cocky Colonels get the idea they could rally. Billy had to be perfect.

That's why Art Welch, the Cascade manager, called time and walked slowly to the mound.

"If you walk him, I want you to pick him off," Art said, nervously smoothing out the dirt on top of the mound with his cleats. "They haven't moved first base in how many years? You're a lefty. Why do you feel the need to look at first base in order to throw there from the stretch? Give it a high leg kick, look home, and throw to first while still looking at home. It's not a balk. It is called memory."

"Art," Billy said.

"Yes?"

"Get the hell off my mound."

With that, Art turned, spat tobacco juice at the grass, and returned to the bench.

If the string of strikeouts persisted, Billy wouldn't have to face the powerful Ducky Holmes until the top of the ninth. As soon as Art left the mound, Billy regained his composure and struck out the side.

The Louisville players seemed confounded by the steady diet of breaking balls. Billy had them swinging from their heels. Each player wished to end the game with the heroism of a titanic home run blast. The Colonels had apparently abandoned the idea of winning the game tactically by simply reaching base, bunting at least one runner into scoring position, and sending the runner dashing for home with the game winning run on a scratch hit through the infield. Apparently, a tactical game plan was beneath the dignity of a big league team facing a team of local rummies. The Colonels were going for broke. They wished to humiliate us with a gargantuan blast. That blast still had not come through eight innings.

In the top of the ninth, the contest would come down to the mighty Ducky Holmes facing a tiring "Steamboat". There were two outs. The Louisville manager did not fear actually losing the game. He didn't want to suffer the embarrassment of a group of amateurs carrying a National League team to extra innings.

The first pitch to Ducky was a fast ball. Billy's pitches were starting to flatten out, losing the customary hop that had frustrated every batter thus far. Ducky stepped out of the batter's box as if to compose himself. He spat into his hands and glanced knowingly at the Louisville manager. I wondered if they believed Billy was finally vulnerable.

He was. The next pitch, a breaking ball, didn't drop off the edge of the table. It hung. Ducky unleashed all of his might on it. The hanging pitch simply spun in the air. The ball lingered there as if to announce itself as a target. Ducky obliged.

He struck the ball with absolute authority. The crack of the bat sent a report to the Cascade mountains. It made something inside of me jump as well.

The ball soared against the sky. I watched its trajectory down the first baseline. It was heading for a place clear of the fence and out in the wilds of Montana beyond the fence.

Ducky tossed his bat aside and arrogantly went straight into his home run trot. He watched the beauty of the ball in flight, as he trotted. We all did.

All eyes were on the ball, the Cascade hopefuls, the Colonels, Ducky, and Billy, too. Billy watched the tragic ending the ball offered, craning his neck to behold its towering flight. The ball absolutely flew toward the right field fence.

Ducky was nearly at first base when the ball suddenly, and inexplicably, hooked foul. The ball had drifted indisputably foul before it cleared the fence. Ducky kicked the dirt near first base in frustration. An audible groan went up from the Louisville bench.

"Foul! Nope!" The home plate umpire ruled in a loud and clear voice, sweeping his extended right arm toward the first base sideline to reinforce his call.

Predictably, Billy fooled Ducky with the next pitch, a breaking ball at the knees. It was strike three. Louisville was out in the top of the ninth.

This left little, if any, realistic chance the game would not progress to extra innings, since Cascade had no real threat in its lineup, and Mullane had breezed through eight innings unscathed. He was ready to face the bottom of our lineup.

The first two Cascade hitters in the bottom of the ninth could scarcely be called hitters. They hadn't as much as fouled off a single pitch in their other at bats. Their performance in the bottom of the ninth was not an exception. They were dismissed by Mullane effortlessly and in order. This left Billy, Cascade's ninth place hitter.

As the pitcher, Billy was not expected to pose any threat to Mullane whatsoever. The Cascade players began picking up their mitts, readying themselves to take the field for extra innings. Billy's at bat was a mere formality. Nevertheless, taking the big league Colonels to extra innings would be a moral victory for Cascade. We had matched a National League team for an entire regulation game. Sure, Billy was already tired, so if the Colonels bombarded him in extra innings, it wouldn't have disappointed anyone's expectations.

The shame in baseball, as in life itself, is not the failure associated with a loss, but the failure to commit the best effort to rage against the probability of loss. Baseball, like life itself, is a game of failure or, more accurately, recovery from failure. The eternal challenge in life, as in baseball, is to learn how to recover from failure.

The rituality of this aspect of the game of baseball is unmistakable. The game of baseball returns each spring as eternally predictable as the earth rotates and the seasons change. Even if Billy failed, and Cascade was defeated, the promise of baseball would remain. It would last to see another spring.

Billy used his cleats to paw at the dirt in the batter's box, digging a hole to anchor his left foot. He held the bat aloft, admired it, spent time organizing his baggy jersey at the collar and over his shoulders, dropped the head of the bat to the plate, tapped the plate twice with the bat, screwed the toe of his left foot in the hole, and held the bat aloft yet again to behold the label, like the Blackfoot girls were expected to adore the statue of the Risen Christ at the Mission. Now, Billy was pronounced ready by the home plate umpire.

Billy remained perfectly still, expectant. The catcher dropped into his crouch. Mullaney looked into home plate for the sign, the catcher's flashing fingers between his knees were shielded by his mitt. Billy didn't need practice swings. On the contrary, he wanted nothing to interfere with his line of sight, his settled focus. It all would happen so fast.

Mullaney accepted the catcher's sign, wound up, and delivered the pitch.

The crack of the bat was solid, but not deafening. Billy had made contact. That, alone, was a victory. He had seen something in Mullaney's delivery that tipped the fast ball, let him know it was coming. The tell allowed Billy to time the pitch perfectly.

Unfortunately, Billy was not known as a power hitter or really a hitter of any kind at all. Even with his best swing, it would take a miracle of Biblical proportion for Billy to even get the ball in play. Nevertheless, this was mere supposition. The facts played out differently on the field.

The ball soared to a surprisingly high elevation. The ball was so high that the only way to track it, really, was against the Montana sky. That ball was indeed in play.

The ball climbed beyond reasonable expectation, vanishing briefly in the white mist of a cloud. The ball wasn't in the clouds. That would have been an exaggeration. It only looked like it was in the clouds. The ball sort of drifted out of the infield and out over the outfield grass, like a mythical God was blowing it to greater heights.

The right fielder tracked it, confidently. He trotted sideways to the far reaches of the park, tracking the ball over his left shoulder, patting his mitt to ready it for the fall of the ball from the glory of its height. The crowd rose, too.

There was the expectation of failure, that the ball would, as usual, somehow descend out of the sky and land safely in the right fielder's waiting mitt, and the folly of those who dared to dream otherwise would be exposed yet again. The right fielder was the last evil that separated the crowd from the mortality of this timeless ambition.

Everyone, the Colonels, the Cascade faithful, and even Billy himself, expected the ball to drop, drop like the flesh is prone to falter at the end of our days. However, there was no fall. Instead, there was only the wonder of flight.

The right fielder could go no farther. He felt for the wall with his outstretched fingers. The wall stopped him from going any farther. He waited. He wondered. He measured the flight of the ball with his eyes, waiting expectantly.

The ball cleared the right field fence and disappeared. It was gone. It was a home run! It was over! The game was over! Cascade had won! The ball was gone forever!

Billy had done the improbable! He hit a massive homerun to win the game! It was over! The game was over!

Cascade had beaten the mighty Louisville Colonels of the National League in the bottom of the ninth inning! The final score: 1-0. The sportswriters would announce the score in bold type across the banner of the newspapers to document what happened here. Cascade: 1 – Louisville: 0. It was over! It was a home run! The game was over!

Billy trotted around the bases as only a hero can. Confident, fluid, slow, and without emotion. He didn't spitefully stab each bag with his cleats on his home run trot. Instead, he seemed to glide over the ground and reverently kiss each passing bag with the souls of his shoes, like a parishioner kisses the ring of a priest.

The crowd turned itself inside out with exuberance. Ordinarily reserved adults jumped, screamed, cried, gawked, danced, and laughed uncontrollably. The Ursuline nuns clasped their hands to cover their mouths. They had witnessed a miracle.

The Louisville side packed up their equipment and said nothing. They would try to erase the experience in Cascade from their minds. However, the school children would not forget. They rushed the diamond to swarm Billy at home plate. He was their hero. He was everybody's hero. The mighty "Steamboat" Billy Wall had blessed Cascade with its finest hour. They would tell the story to their children and to their grandchildren across the generations. Cascade had challenged the mighty Colonels of the National League and won.

Chapter Twenty

Cascade, Montana, May 1913

I had tears in my eyes remembering Billy. Those glory years were gone forever. There would never be another Billy. He was an aberration that occurred once in a lifetime, if you were lucky.

Frankly, I was embarrassed to be in tears over a stupid baseball game. I had let the *Cascade Courier* reporter in on an enormous secret. After all of these years, I still had a girlish crush on the divinely gifted "Steamboat" Billy Wall. It was natural. Everyone did. He was much more than a man.

Thinking back, Billy was larger than life. Baseball. Montana. The Pacific Northwest. The railroad. If any of these things loomed larger than "Steamboat" Billy Wall, Billy must have been a mighty close second.

"What did you think of Steamboat, Mary?" The reporter grinned.

"Steamboat?"

"Yes."

"Steamboat was the second coming of Christ as far as I could tell, the best I'd ever seen. Is that clear? You had a better chance of fooling Mother Nature than hitting Billy's fast ball. He could knock over a brick wall with it and pick the brick."

"Did Steamboat ever make it to the majors?"

"Does it matter?" I said, angered. "Doesn't matter one way

or the other. When Christ rose from the dead, there was nothing else He needed to do, except remember it. Do you think He had to rise from the dead a second time, or was once enough?"

"You have a point there. What did you do after this legendary contest?"

"I handed out flowers. That's what I did after every game. Each player who did something special got a flower for his jersey button. Players who got a hit or made a nice catch or a great throw got flowers. But for players who hit home runs, I gave away an entire bouquet. Billy got all of the flowers that day. He pitched a no-hitter, hit the game winning home run, and he did it against the vaunted Louisville Colonels of the National League. He will be remembered in the lore of Montana and the entire Pacific Northwest forever."

"Did you really punch that sportswriter before the game?"

"No."

We both laughed.

"Of course, I did. The fellow had it coming to him. I don't want to brag or make you think I was a hot head, but anytime some fellow criticized any of my boys on the team I tended to get a little miffed. This *reporter*, as you called him—but frankly, I am not sure what exactly he was—the fellow had a big mouth. Imagine you are visitors at a ball field in Montana, or anywhere in the nation really, and you are visiting from the National League. Even the words, National League, have magic in them. The National League is supposed to be something you only read about in the newspapers. You don't ever think you'd actually get the chance to play a National League team. Well, Cascade got its chance. That's a big deal. Everyone in these parts thought it was a big deal, because it was a big deal. Everyone looks up to major league ball players. The chance to actually play one, to measure your skill against the best there is, is a dream come true, don't you think? Now you have to understand, the fellow was a reporter or scout or someone associated with a big league ball club out here in the middle of Montana playing a town team. You got to know that is a big deal to the locals. Instead of showing a little class, you shoot off your big mouth and believe you can get away with it? No chance. Not in Montana, not in the great Pacific Northwest, not anywhere."

"I'll accept that answer as a yes," the reporter said, smirking.

"I don't care how you take the answer as long as there is the promise of a stiff drink and a fat cigar at the end of it. I never missed a game.

"While I was running the Star Route, I was also doing laundry, cooking food, babysitting, staging cat fights on Halloween, not actual cats of course. I would dress up in black and paint my face like a cat, get on my hands and knees, and face another person dressed like a cat, start pawing and hissing. The kids loved it, and so did I.

"There was getting to be a lot of action around town, too. There was a ferry across the Missouri River and a new railroad stop. This was bringing a lot of strangers to town. Put the strangers together with the Copperheads, the Crow and the Blackfeet, and we were starting to get somewhere. Now, where we were actually going was open to conjecture. The point is we were going, like the rest of the nation was going.

"There was an assay office, a bank, a couple of saloons, and a couple of whorehouses to take care of all this going we were doing. Cascade was on the move. We were growing. We were not being left behind by the rest of the nation."

"Where exactly were you in life at the time Cascade played

the Colonels?"

"Hell, I was technically an old lady at this stage, but I never let on that I was old. Why would I? I just kept delivering the mail and getting paid for it. That was far easier said than done. The Star Route was hard work, and it was dangerous work."

Chapter Twenty-One

Montana Territory, January 1903

The mail train into Miles City, Butte, Billings, Helena, and Great Falls was never late. The blizzards didn't change anything. The mail run had to go on. It didn't get a vacation, take a sick day, or stay at home due to inclement weather.

During one particularly bad storm, I remember pulling on two pair of men's wool trousers, two overcoats, two hats, and snowshoes. I needed the snowshoes to walk on top of the snow drifts, which were over ten feet high at the time, and those snow drifts seem to get higher and higher the more often I tell the story! I had to climb over the snow to get to the barn.

In the barn, I hitched the team. The horses stood compliant, well-fed, well-groomed, and their stalls had been mucked out the night before. I was ready to face the snows of a particularly cruel blizzard.

The horses snorted. Thankfully, I didn't hear any coughing. The immensity of the beasts raised the temperature in the barn considerably. However, the warmth and comfort created by their body heat was erased the instant I threw open the barn door. Then, the wind and the snow had its way with us.

I rubbed the velvet faces of each horse in the swirling wind. In turn, each beast tossed its head lovingly. My horses craved attention. I offered the rubbery lips of each horse an apple from the palm of my hand.

I commanded the horses to halt. They complied, standing erect, motionless. My mule, Moses, scowled at me from his stall. He felt betrayed. He was not invited to the party. He might have felt like part of the team, but he wasn't. He was lucky to be able to wait out the storm from the protection of the barn.

The horses would have plenty to do just to brave the going through the snow. We were on a deadline. We were off, leaving behind the fires of home still burning in the field stone fireplace, a roasting, comforting fire that was so inviting and so very hard to leave. Nevertheless, we did leave. Duty called.

The horses showed courage lifting their knees high above the snow drifts to keep the stagecoach moving. There were times when the drifting snow was as high as the horses' shoulders. That is when the stagecoach slowed to nearly a halt. I stood up on the box and gave the team their heads by dropping the reins. The team carried on, urging the stagecoach forward, clearing snow drift after snow drift.

With the sky turning grey with the coming of dawn, we reached a passable opening. It was a regular roadbed, no rocks, breaks, or crevices. It would be smooth going all the way to the railroad stop from there.

I shook the reins and screamed at the team. I let them know who was boss. The team responded. Their ears twitched. They snorted and bowed their necks, trotting, picking up the pace. The harnesses sang with the effort.

I turned to light a cigar. That's when I spotted a figure emerging from the grey curtain of dawn. It had stopped snowing, but the wind still made it difficult to hear. The figure looked like a man standing in our path. The horses stopped, refusing to confront the stranger.

I climbed off the box, careful to hold my shotgun at the

ready. I ran my free hand cautiously along the reins and then the bridles. I patted the faces of several of the horses to reassure them everything was in hand.

"Easy boys," I whispered.

However, the horses were still nervous, fearful. They snorted. They complained. They were skittish on their hooves. They sensed danger.

I slowly walked toward the figure. It was the size of a man, but I couldn't figure out why a man would be out alone in the storm without a horse, even if he was a bandit trying to rob the stagecoach.

"Who goes there?" I warned.

There was no reply.

I sized up the figure as I planted my check over the lock plate of the Winchester and looked down the barrel. I sighted the target and walked forward in that position, careful not to disturb my aim.

"I say, who goes there?"

There was no reply. There was only the noise of the wind. It grabbed my scarf.

I kept walking. I wasn't wearing my snowshoes. There was no need for snowshoes. The snow was not deep on the road.

I got within a few feet of the figure. Then, it dawned on me. It wasn't a man.

It was a black grizzly bear. I could see the girth and the rough silhouette of fur. I could see its cubs walking there, too. The bear was in search of food. It was bitterly cold.

On the prairie, there is no wisdom in charity. There is wisdom in foresight. There is wisdom in domination. There is wisdom in determination.

I broke off a round. The report echoed against the Cascades. This angered the bear. The cubs scampered away.

I broke off another round. This time I aimed closer to the target. The round must have breezed pretty close to the business part of the grizzly. It turned and vanished, ambling off on all fours.

Suddenly, a wolf attacked me from the rear. I saw only flashing teeth. I could hear the snarling desperation of the wolf, but I couldn't react to the attack. I couldn't see it. The wolf had succeeded in ambushing me. It was a complete surprise.

I wheeled. Instinctively, I kicked at the wolf's teeth. I couldn't orient the long gun. I couldn't get the barrel down in time. I couldn't shoot it. The shotgun was too long. The wolf was too close.

Instead of firing the gun, I swung the barrel of the shotgun to ward off the attack. I tried to hit the wolf with the barrel of the gun. It didn't work.

The wolf growled and yelped. The wolf jumped lustily after my long overcoat. Fortunately, I was wearing two pairs of wool trousers.

The layers of wool saved me from the cruelty of the wolf's sharp teeth. If those teeth so much as nipped me, opened flesh, and drew blood, I could have gotten sick swiftly with rabies — or worse.

"Get! You sonofabitch! Hah! Get! Get!" I screamed.

The screams forced the wolf backward ever so slightly. I turned the shotgun over and swung the butt of the shotgun again and again wildly. This time, I managed to connect with the wolf's skull.

The wolf jumped at me in retaliation. I swung again and again. The wolf tried to bite the butt of the shotgun.

I swung wildly. The butt cracked solid bone. This made the wolf recoil. I aimed the shotgun. I fired. The round may have hit the wolf. I wasn't sure. If I hit the wolf, it couldn't have been a direct hit, or there would have been silence. There wasn't silence. There was the sound of the wolf yelping, retreating into the swiftly approaching dawn.

"Must have grazed him," I mumbled.

I rejoined the team. The horses looked at me dumbly through the slits in their blinkers. They tossed their heads as if to agree with the outcome. I could hear the breast plates, collars, hame chains, bits, and other parts of the harnesses singing.

We arrived at the railroad stop, early. The train wasn't due to arrive for another hour. We waited the hour. Finally, I heard the train was clanging and banging in the distance. The whistle howled against the Cascades. Then, I could see it belching black smoke. The smoke, and the hiss of steam, reminded me of my days aboard the Robert E. Lee on the Mississippi River.

Thinking back, I grew secretly emotional as I reminisced about the Robert E. Lee. The conductors hopped down from the train, as it eased into the station. There were no passengers.

There was only freight. I signed paperwork, took custody of the mail bags, and loaded the stagecoach.

Invariably, the mail bags contained important legal documents, currency, newspapers, letters, stuff like that. The stagecoach was a bandit's dream. However, as long as I had the Star Route, the dream would quickly become a bandit's nightmare. I had the .38, the Winchester, the cigar, the whiskey flask, and six feet and two hundred pounds of bad attitude. I was steadfast in ensuring that the mail's chain of custody was not broken. If the mail delivery was unreliable, it would stunt the growth of the entire region.

I owed a duty to Cascade to deliver the mail without fail. I intended to exercise that duty with expert care and unfailing courage. In over eight years of service to the United States Postal Service, I never failed once. I was never late to meet a single train. I never missed a single day of work due to illness or inclement weather. I didn't lose a single load to bandits, thieves, wolves, or bears. This record speaks for itself.

The return trip wasn't memorable. There were no wolves, no grizzly bears, no bandits, and no problems. I dropped off the mail in Cascade without further incident. Surprisingly, I was to confront the steepest challenge of my life upon my return home.

Chapter Twenty-Two

Fire!

My clapboard house was engulfed in flames! The fire raged over the roof, lashing everything in its reach.

The flames roared and popped and crackled, licking the walls, the roof, everywhere. I could see through the windows that other flames were having their way with the inside of the house, too. They had turned it into an inferno. The orange and blue and yellow flames illuminated everything.

I snapped the whip at the horses. The stagecoach hopped over the rough going. I raced away from the house looking for help.

I screamed to get the neighboring rancher's attention. The rancher and the ranch hands came running. They hopped in the stagecoach. The horses seemed to sense the urgency. They got after their business in earnest.

We turned onto my land on two wheels. I drove the team straight into the barn. I didn't want to endanger the horses. Horses do odd things in a fire, like rush into flames to their death seeking protection in what they consider instinctually to be the safety of their home even though their home happens also to be on fire.

I left the team hitched to the stagecoach. I slammed the barn door. The boys sprinted to the house.

We formed a bucket brigade. The buckets of water were passed from hand-to-hand, from man-to-man, down the line. The man at the front of the line fought the flames. He threw as much water as he had. He fought gallantly. There were many buckets of water expended in the fight.

The flames fought back. They popped and snapped. The insatiable hunger of that inferno searched every inch of the house for dry wood. The heat was intense. It snatched the breath from my lungs.

The water from the buckets made small parts of the inferno gasp, object. The buckets earned small victories. However, the victories were temporary. The fight raged on. Suddenly, the wind whispered. This made the flames leap even higher with delight, almost as though the dancing flames taunted us.

We ignored the danger. The buckets kept coming. There were no organized fire patrols in those years. There was simply the bond of humanity.

The flames unlocked something mysterious, primal. They spurred the men to action. This is why we fought. We fought to save something, anything of my history, the part of my history that possessions symbolized. We tried to hang on to the past. Instead of saving what was left of my home, I watched it all vanish. The light of that evil illuminated the faces of the men.

I was resigned to this fate. I was strangely mesmerized by the ravenous flames. I watched them dance and taunt.

The wind grew stiff, and then fierce. This fueled the ambitious flames to insurmountable heights. The heat threw the men backward. The bucket line was pitiful by comparison. Everything was lost.

In the morning, the sunshine revealed the damage. My home had been reduced to a charred and still smoldering pile of rubble. The few blackened boards and planks that remained upright disgusted me, like the bones of a roasted hog picked clean at a holiday feast.

Chapter Twenty-Three

Cascade, Montana, May 1913

The reporter didn't dare speak. He let me gather my thoughts. I was on the verge of tears yet again. Then, he did the work of a news reporter.

"How did you survive the ordeal of your home perishing in the fire?'

"The people of Cascade threw me a life-line, was how. I was extremely well-liked. I fed them when they were hungry and went out of business doing it. I laundered their clothes. I treated them when they were sick. I babysat their children. I supported their baseball teams."

"You knocked out their enemies," the reporter laughed.

"I broke more noses than anyone in the great Pacific Northwest. I once shot a man in the buttocks for calling me a nigger!"

We both laughed.

"Back to the fire," the reporter redirected the focus, avoiding the topic of racial slurs.

"The way we bonded, the folks of Cascade. This didn't happen overnight, and of course they might not invite you into their homes for dinner, but they welcomed me into their saloons for whiskey. That was quite enough for me."

"Seems like it was."

"It was. Remember, I was the only lady allowed in a saloon

in those days. They made an exception for me. Anyway, back to the fire."

"Please."

"Yes, the folks got together and raised a new house for me in about two days. They laid the foundation, set the floor, raised the frames and beams, capped the roof, and closed the walls. It was the miracle of people working together toward a common goal. My new house was better than the old one, frankly. Of course, I could not replace the heirlooms and other personal items that are timeless, like photographs. But it all worked out quite well in the end."

"Did they build the new house on the very spot where the old house burned down?'

"Yes."

"Back to baseball, what exactly did you do after beating the Louisville Colonels?

"We went to the saloon and got drunk. We threw back so many shots of whiskey, sang so many songs, and I even got to dance with Billy."

"Describe that."

"Describe that! Billy was every woman's dream come true. He was a knight in shining armor, like the knights of King Arthur's roundtable, except a knight with a nasty fast ball. It was the best time I ever had in a saloon—and I had me some wonderful times in saloons—yes, sir, indeed."

"The mail runs."

"Treacherous. The mail runs were treacherous. The winters out here are sub-zero with wind and snow, drifting snow, and the blizzards don't stop the trains or the mail. The mail never stops. It is the life blood of how the country grows. It can't be stopped. To stop it is to stop the country's heart from beating. I had a contract to honor. Thank God for Sister Amadeus. She put me on to the contract, set me up with the team and the stagecoach. It was her vision. She made it all happen."

"Yes, but none of it would have happened unless you had the skill to do the job."

"It was a job for two men, actually. I was only one woman. The route is not even a real route. It is ground you got to drive the team over. It is rocky. It has dips and breaks, crevices, mountain climbs, and there is some easy going over cattle drives. It is freezing in the winter. It is blazing hot in the summer. The reason it is a job for two men is the second man is needed to brandish the shotgun needed discourage the bandits and Indians from sticking up the stagecoach."

"By the way, I'll bet Sister Amadeus thanked God for *you*. You saved her life."

"We saved each other's lives."

"If the job of the stage run on the Star Route was a job for two men, how did you do it alone?"

"I did it alone because I am six feet tall, carry two guns, and don't mind a good fight. That's how. I carry the Winchester, the .38, and a nasty disposition along with me wherever I go. That's how I made good on my promise to deliver the mail. I fought off attacks from bears, wolves, Irishmen, Mexicans, and Poles. And I did it for a very long time, too."

"How long?"

"Eight years."

"And what was your family life like?"

"Family?"

"Yes, family."

"Never did have much of a family. You have to remember, I didn't get off the plantation back in Tennessee until I was already in my thirties. Never did have much of a family life. Didn't even know my exact birth date."

"Cascade celebrates your birthday every year. Kids take the day off from school."

"Yes, and that shows Cascade is my real family, doesn't it? Some years, I tell them to celebrate two days! Why stop at one?"

This time, the laughter reached out into the rest of the newsroom.

The other writers sort of watched the interview out of the corner of their eyes instead of fully concentrating on their assignments. I must have seemed odd to them, an old lady wearing a long dress over twenty years out of fashion, a very black lady smoking a homemade cigar. I must have seemed like a living monument to the past.

"Anyway," I said without prompting, "Montana wasn't even a state yet. That didn't come until much later. Actually, Cascade wasn't even an incorporated town yet, either, so there was some question about the laws out here. For example, I know the town was called Ulidia before it became Cascade. The Town of Cascade wasn't incorporated until 1877. That was just before I got out here to the Mission from Ohio. There basically wasn't nothing out here in Montana back then except Blackfoot and Crow Indians, Copperheads, and ranchers. The copper miners would come later."

"What's a Copperhead?"

"A Copperhead is a Confederate. The Copperheads were known for fighting on the Confederate side during the Civil War. Mr. Lincoln won the Civil War. He tried to make up with the South afterwards to keep the Union alive and growing. He basically let these guys roam around out here and not give up their ways. All they had to do to get back into the good graces of the federal government was to take an oath to uphold the Constitution. That was it! And I remember how it felt during the Civil War. It wasn't that long ago. Back on the plantation in Tennessee, we got word about the campaigns, the battles, the casualties, the steady advance of the Union troops to the sea the same way it came to everyone else. It came in glimpses from what was written in letters, reported in old newspapers, assuming we were lucky enough to get an old newspaper, and the stories people who had read newspapers and letters told us about the war. That was it. Our imaginations played a role in its eventual reality.

"And, of course, there was always the chance the Civil War might visit you at your doorstep. Back then, that kind of scared you to think about it. I know you didn't ask me about the Civil War, but it was really the only thing on our minds back on the plantation.

"The colored troops made us proud to be colored during the campaign. The 26th Colored Regiment had its battle flag and wore the colors of the federal government. Think of it. The 26th went out and got us our revenge. Those colored soldiers won revenge on the battlefield. If we had nothing else to show for the years we were enslaved—and it seemed like the nation was determined that we would never get anything to show for those years of slavery—we at least got our revenge."

The thought of the 26th made my voice quiver. I paused. I was nearly in tears. I decided right then and there to take command of the interview, like seizing the reins of a team of horses hitched to a stagecoach.

"I am going to tell you the reports we heard about the 26th and Mr. Lincoln's courage," I said, looking deeply into the reporter's eyes. "Whether Mr. Lincoln's plan would succeed came down to what happened on the battlefield. You have to remember, we were still enslaved people on a plantation in Hickman County, Tennessee. I remember it like it was yesterday. It was terrifying."

Chapter Twenty-Four

The reporter fell into a stunned silence. Most folks did, actually, when anyone who lived through the war was ready to talk about it. His eyeballs were magnified to sheer enormity by the thick lenses of his eyeglasses.

"Reports of the war changed me in ways I never would have believed possible," I said, looking out across the newsroom.

"How could the war move you so deeply if you only heard reports about it and didn't actually see a real battle?"

"Oh, I wouldn't say it was the battles that changed my outlook. I would say it was what came *after* the battles. You see, I found out about that firsthand from the people who were there. See, I knew two boys who had joined up with the 26th, one of the colored regiments. Some of the colored soldiers acquitted themselves on the battlefield, but others were only given servile roles, like tending to the horses, cooking, helping out around the hospital tents, and digging graves.

"I happened to know a couple of soldiers who were given the job of digging holes on the battlefield after one side had retreated. They were given the job of working on the battlefields long after the battles were over. One of the boys was a lanky negro from Missouri. Nobody quite gathered how he came to join up with the 26th instead of one of the volunteer units closer to his home. Anyway, he was real quiet, odd.

Didn't say much about himself, ever. The boys in his regiment eventually managed after a few months to get him to say his name, Edmund Bouchard.

"Missouri told me later that everyone in the 26th thought Bouchard was a comical name for a slave, but weren't quite sure why it sounded comical. He said when he was asked if he was free or a fugitive, he ignored the question altogether. The other colored soldiers took a liking to him, so they decided to take the liberty of giving him a nickname, Missouri.

"I met him after the war. I only knew him by his nickname—Missouri—nothing else. I thought he was odd, too. Anyway, he took a liking to me, and he was really the only man I remember who ever cared about me one way or the other, to tell the God's honest truth."

"Was he your boyfriend?"

"It never got that far. He didn't seem to know how to make it go that far if those really were his intentions, or maybe it was the war that took away most of what was supposed to be inside of him. I don't know. He told me he was a soldier, but he didn't get the chance to fight. But when the fighting was over, he said he was one of the two boys assigned the duty of burying the dead. He told me this in a very strange way. He didn't really ever look directly at me while he told me the stories. He looked at me sideways. He stared off toward nowhere, like he was seeing what happened to him all over again in his head. It was really so odd, all of it. He told the story in a way that made me see it, too. I believe that's why it hit me so hard."

"What did he say that made it seem so real?"

"He said the next day after the battle, the battlefield was crowded with the gore of dead bodies, Union and Confederate alike. Most of the men were faced downward. Those were the easy ones to move. He said he didn't have to look at their faces, as he dragged those bodies by their limbs that were made dumb by death, limp and flopping around at strange angles. He said he could turn those bodies over without looking at them and roll them into the holes. But he said the other bodies, the bodies that faced the sky, were the hard ones to move. He had to look at the shocking looks on their horrified faces. He said the flies were busy at most of the bodies that were swollen in death well beyond their normal sizes. The smell was oppressive.

"It would get worse the higher the sun rose in the sky and the hotter the afternoon became, so he said he worked as fast as he could to finish the job. There were guts on the ground here and there, exposed and baking in the sun. He said there were always two boys assigned to do the work. They'd cover their mouths and noses with handkerchiefs like bandits, but the stench penetrated the cloth. There was nothing they could do except work fast. They dug holes eight to ten feet long, and they rolled as many bodies as possible into each hole. He said they were careful to follow orders not to drop Union and Confederate soldiers into the same hole."

"Did he ever tell you what happened out on the battlefield?" the reporter asked, pulling off his eyeglasses.

"They had a war," I deadpanned.

"I know. I mean what happened exactly during the battles to make so many casualties? Did you find out?" The reporter wiped the lenses of his eyeglasses with a white handkerchief.

"I guess I was never interested in asking him about things like that—battle tactics, which side had the other side outnumbered, or anything else about rifle pits, bridges, creeks, swamps, woods, federal tactics, federal formations or rebel tactics and rebel formations, or anything else you might ask about battles. I really didn't care none about any of that. All I could think about was how the dead were left behind on the battlefield long after it was all over, and well after the sun had risen the next day, and how all that was left after the battle was the sun and the flies and no real explanation for why the men were dead.

"The sky was still wonderfully beautiful over the dead the next day, but Missouri still had his orders to roll the Union and Confederate bodies into separate holes. I guess the emptiness of that story tended to mess with your mind if you thought about it too long."

"You never did figure it out, did you?" the reporter asked.

"Figure out what? You should have asked me whether I asked Missouri whether *he* figured it out. He was there. He was the fellow doing the digging."

"Did you ask him?"

"Yes, and the answer he gave is one of the reasons his story hit me so hard. The way he told it he said he once really tried to figure it all out. He was working with another boy, digging holes. Missouri said he stopped work to rub the sweat off his brow with the back of his wrist, stood over his shovel, and looked out over the battlefield toward the horizon. He said he had been digging all day. By then, the sky was streaked with the orange of sunset. He said he rested for a minute or two. Both he and the other boy stopped work at the same time, so there was no noise. He said he looked at the boy to see if he wanted to talk. The boy didn't say a word. Then, Missouri said he really began to think about things when they started digging again, and this time, he didn't bother making eye contact and didn't try to talk to the boy. It was understandable. The boy hadn't said anything intelligent the entire time they were digging."

"What happened next?"

"Missouri said he began to preach to the other boy. He told the boy that they can dig as many holes as they want, but the souls of the dead live on as surely as the sun sets and rises. He said he had thought about the question a long while and warmed up to an explanation. The other boy stopped digging to listen to the explanation. Missouri said he told the boy that if the soul ever lives, it must live in a place like this. They can kill the body on this field, but they can't kill the soul any more than they can kill love or hope, or sorrow or hate."

"Did you ask Missouri if he told the boy what he meant by that?"

"Yes, I did. Missouri really didn't look at me as he answered, but…he answered."

"What did he say?"

"Missouri said he didn't give the boy an explanation, and the boy didn't ask for one. Missouri said there wasn't anything else to say about it, anyway. Instead of talking, he said they just kept digging."

Chapter Twenty-Five

I needed time to recover. I remembered the letters and newspaper stories about the war vividly. Our humanity was at stake.

The news reporter gave me time. He knew how deep sentiments about the Civil War ran for those who lived through it. He wisely switched to a less controversial topic. It was only right.

We began to reconsider my early days in Montana, the one place on earth that had captured my admiration. I knew the history of the place quite well.

The federal government had decided not to interfere in the affairs of the Territories, aside from guaranteeing a narrow strip of land to the railroads. Everything else was fair game. It was wild.

The stagecoach lines covered treacherous going. The railroad and the ferry would eventually inspire dramatic change. Of course, Sister Amadeus founded the Ursuline Convent of the Sacred Heart, a school for Blackfoot girls just outside of the Cascade town limits. Montana was certainly a major part of the ambitious Western expansion.

"You know, I often wondered why. Why would the Jesuits come all the way out here to form a school?" the reporter asked.

"Oh, that was very important to the Catholics. It was a way of life for them. It was a way for them to spread the Word of God. The Jesuits were above all missionaries. Don't forget that, but forming the school was also a way for them to help the country evolve."

"How so?"

"They figured if they could make the girls Catholics, when the girls became mothers, they would raise their children as Catholics, and the Blackfeet would become less hostile to the idea of evolution and the railroad and the white man coming out here, progress, the westward spread of the nation. You have to admit, it worked."

"I suppose you could call it a form of progress."

"I suppose you're right. Anyway, we were a growing town, area really. The copper miners started speculating out here. The ranchers basically were always out here. The ferry across the Missouri River brought new folks out this way. They opened up a bank, assay office, and two saloons, and of course they had a couple of whorehouses open up when things got going good around here, one of them was a place called Fat Jack's, believe it or not."

"Fat Jack's."

"Let's see, we talked about the baseball team already. The team was a major part of our identity, our pride, who we were as a town."

"Clearly."

"I recorded more knockouts in Montana than anyone, ranchers, farmers, miners, Copperheads, it didn't matter. They popped off at the mouth. They get dropped. Heck, I was beginning to wonder whether any of these boys out here could fight. I was wondering if they ever heard of the idea of practice. Yes, practice. Take a boxing lesson or two if you can't fight, for example. Then, you get the idea of the science. Hell, don't just take a broken nose and the humiliation that comes with it lightly. There is more to the idea of knocking out a rancher than just throwing back enough whiskey to gain courage. It is a science. *Science.*"

"A science? What do you mean, a science?"

"A science in the sense that you measure a fellow before you decide to knock him out."

"How do you take those kinds of measurements?"

"First, I look at the size of the hands, the mitts. If a fellow has oversized mitts, you'd best leave him alone. Now, on the other hand, if the guy has little girlie hands, no matter how big his frame, I have no problem trading punches with him. He can't hurt me with a punch even if he lands, and the chances are that he isn't going to land in the first place. So, the first tip is the hands."

"Of course, I bet you had to make sure to watch the hands to make sure he wasn't drawing."

"That stuff about drawing in Montana was seriously overrated. Everybody thinks it was that wild out here as in gunfights and duels and stickups every day, the Wild West you read about in books. Hell, it was wild out here, but it wasn't that damn wild. Besides, everybody had a gun in those days, so there was no sense in drawing unless you really were serious about using the gun. It just never was that serious. Seriously, there were bandits, thieves, stagecoach robbers, and hostile Sioux and Cheyenne, but it was rare anybody had a problem with a gun, very rare. That stuff about Montana was purely theatrical. Now, Oklahoma, Indian Territory at the time, now that may have been an entirely different story."

"Unless, of course, someone decided to shoot someone else in the buttocks." The reporter was making jokes, very entertaining.

"That was a charity shooting. I hope that guy didn't take it personally, but I bet he learned his lesson about racial slurs, think? That stuff about Montana being wild with gunplay and shootouts and bank robberies was purely theatrical. Hell, it was a long time before we even saw our first bank out here. How do you rob a bank that ain't there? Now, Oklahoma may have been an entirely different story. They was really wild in Oklahoma, barely civilized."

We laughed. I matched him joke for joke.

"Why pick on Oklahoma?"

"I ain't picking on Oklahoma. It wasn't even Oklahoma at the time. It was Cherokee and Creek Nation in what was known as Indian Territory. There was Arkansas across the border, Fort Smith, places like that, at least that's what was written in the newspapers we got out here. The railroad inched its way across Indian Territory the same way it inched its way out here, except Montana is far more rocky and treacherous territory than Oklahoma. Anyway, back to the fighting rules. You know what my second rule on fighting was?"

"No, tell me."

"Never fight a little fellow. The little fellows have been proving themselves in fights from the time they was yea high." I extended the palm of my hand, indicating diminutive size. "Them boys will trade if you look at them wrong. They throw. They throw gladly. They throw wildly. They get practice fighting. The reason is fellows look at their size, get it twisted, and then want to take them on.

"The second rule is, don't fight little guys, unless you really are looking to have a fight on your hands. Now, big guys, on the other hand—big guys usually can't fight at all. The reason is they never get no practice, so they never get good at it. The size discourages fellows from taking them on. They get by just on intimidating folks with their size. They never have to prove themselves. I'll fight a big fellow any day of the week."

"Okay."

"Do you want to know the third and final rule about fighting?"

"Yes."

"There are no rules. That is the third rule of fighting. There are no rules, so there is no such thing as a fair fight. There are only fights. That is the third rule of fighting."

"Sounds about right for the West."

"Sounds about right for anywhere. This stuff is in the soul of the nation. It goes into what makes it tick."

"What?"

"The concept that you go out and get it done on your own. You overcome the bitter cold of the winter on your own. If your friend is stricken with pneumonia, you don't call a doctor. There are no doctors for over sixty miles. And if you got one, they don't know no cure for pneumonia any better than you do. So, you best find a way to cure it yourself, or there is a grave site somewhere with your name written on it, right? Death was a constant visitor in Montana.

"They called us pioneers. You needed a house to live in, you built it yourself. If you didn't know how to build a house, you weren't likely to ever have anyone to come along to build it for you.

"You needed to build a Mission, run stagecoach, you got it done yourself, or it didn't get done. That's what's inside the soul of the nation. I believe that is what they meant when they called us pioneers. The nation might have looked down its nose at us, but we are part of its soul. The soul lives in a place like Montana, a place off in the middle of nowhere. While we were still one of the territories, we were already here before there technically was a here. It is funny to look at it this way, isn't it? If you lived through it, you might think of it this way. In a way, we are in a type of eternal childhood that promises to forgive us for who we truly are no matter how badly we behave. This explains why the nation is halfway invulnerable. In the case of the Louisville Colonels, Mullane's vulnerability that day was tipping his fast ball. Billy waited for it. He got it. Like Billy hitting a home run, the only way anything gets done in Montana is if you do it yourself."

"And when you needed to fight, you got that done on your own, too, right? Any particularly memorable occasions you can think of when you used any of the rules to get into a really good fight?"

Now, that question really got me thinking. There were a few fights that were memorable. The time I knocked out the sportswriter traveling with the Louisville Colonels was one, but there were others.

Chapter Twenty-Six

Cascade, Montana, April 1903

I was playing poker at the Silver Dollar saloon. I was sitting at a table across from two other hands. The first fellow was a little guy from Texas. He was about the same size as a tree stump, give or take a few inches. His partner, a fellow who went by the name of Jack, was a lumbering sort, the kind you find out on the prairie angrily tossing around hay or cursing wildly while insisting with brute force that a steer do something, anything, the steer didn't have a mind to do.

The boys must have already spent hours in the saloon that day, even before the card game got going.

They talked with slurred speech as though they were drinking laudanum instead of whiskey. Furthermore, the short fellow from Texas spoke like he had two tongues in his mouth and hadn't bothered to organize them before leaving his house that morning.

I was holding three of a kind in my hand, three Queens. I was waiting to spring the trap.

"Tex, s'it looks like da lady're got us beat this han'," Jack said.

"Lady! Lady? T'ain't no lady, Jake," Tex said, looking at the table like the table was the deck of a ship floating on a troubled sea. "Wassah madder with chu? You never could hold whiskey. That's a man! I tell you...Jake."

"Tis so, a lady, a big ole colored lady."

"T'ain't really no such thing as a colored lady, colored *girl*, maybe, but t'ain't no colored *ladies*, not where I'm from anyway."

"Where you're from! T'ain't been established where the devil you're from to my satisfaction anyway. You ain't no better…"

I slapped my cards face up on the table.

"Three of a kind, boys. Don't matter what you call me, actually. Matters what I *am*. And right about now *I'm* the *winner*. Pay up."

"You mean'ah tell me yuh bin sittin' at this table and yuh didn't know yuh was sittin' 'cross from a lady, Tex?" Jack persisted, hiccupping.

"There it is 'gin. No matter how many times you say it. I got no problem with yuh," Tex said, looking across the saloon. "I got a problem with, with, with, with them boys over there or nothing else." Tex stood up. He adjusted his belt. He sat back done.

"Where yah goin' Tex?" Jack asked.

"Nowhere."

"One of you better be going somewhere, like out to get my money, unless you got it on you," I implored.

Tex looked at me like he couldn't believe his ears, like he possibly was looking at neither a lady nor a man, but a monster. He exaggerated opening his eyes wide, so more white than usual showed. Then, he squinted, like there wasn't enough light in the room.

He avoided eye contact by looking across the saloon at the bartender.

He did this to give himself enough time to figure out what to do about the colored lady before him. The bartender kept working the bar, setting up glass shot glasses, pouring whiskey.

Then, it happened.

Tex knocked over the table trying to get at me. He swung wildly. I caught the punch, grabbed it out of the midair.

The part that infuriated Tex is that I not only caught the punch, I held it and subdued him. That is, I held onto his fist with one hand. He couldn't overcome my strength to free it. He swung with his free hand. I blocked that blow.

When I got tired of blocking blows, I hit Tex with a left hook that glanced off his nose. However, I caught enough of his nose to draw blood. There was a lot of blood, too.

The sight of blood has a way of revealing character. It presents something of an emotional crossroads. There is one road that requires you to stand your ground, to fight. There is another road that offers a way out of your troubles, the one that offers escape to the fleet of foot. Tex elected to pick the later. So, he didn't bother picking up the table. He fled through the saloon doors and vanished!

"And if you want the rest of it, wait for me outside," I yelled pointlessly at the saloon doors, which were now closed.

I looked at Jack. He was stunned. He hadn't come to the aid of his friend. He hadn't risen from his chair. In fact, he hadn't done anything at all. He just sat there.

"You want some of this, too, partner?" I asked, leaning close enough to Jack to give him a kiss.

Wisely, Jack didn't answer. He simply ran.

The memorable part of the incident was none of the boys in the saloon saw the need to intervene. They knew my reputation. They knew I packed power in both hands.

After sunset, the ranch hands came into town from the prairie. They hitched their horses at the rail. Most nights, the saloon got crowded and rowdy after sunset. I was at home in all of that action.

Chapter Twenty-Seven

Cascade, Montana, May 1913

The reporter was interested in talking about the perils of prairie life back before the railroads got going. He talked about gold, boisterous railroad towns, ranching, farming, homesteading, copper mines, and the rest of the panorama associated with the Western expansion, like I was a historian, an authority, or something. I wanted to talk about how the women's suffrage amendment to the state constitution finally passed that year, and how the perils of life on the Western frontier sped up the recognition of women's rights, but this didn't seem to tickle the reporter's fancy.

Women's suffrage didn't appear to be a topic the reporter had written anywhere in his notes. He was after a more sensational story, something that would sell newspapers. In his view, women's rights simply wouldn't sell.

I knew the reporter wanted to talk about Indians.

The reporter wanted to know if I had any close calls with any of the tribal nations. Now, a story about a woman running mail out in the middle of nowhere may show some appeal, but if the story is complicated by the woman repelling an attack by hostile Indians, now, that was a story that would sell newspapers. Unfortunately, I couldn't oblige the reporter's sense of intrigue. However, there were a couple of incidents involving Indians who rode up to my stagecoach out of nowhere.

The stage run went across the open prairie between Cascade and Billings. There were all sorts of perils, surprises. However, the United States Postal Service didn't insure against surprises, Indian attacks, or anything else, really. You were strictly on your own.

The Crow was the first tribe to confront me. I wasn't worried at all. The reason is it was broad daylight. I could see the riders coming up out of the distance. I could tell they were not bandits. I could tell they were Crow by the way they rode.

The riders leaned into the necks of their ponies, busy bouncing in their saddles. There were no irons, so their lanky legs curled across the bellies of the ponies, like ropes. The riders wore skirts over their loins, not trousers. The skirts sported colorful patterns, including rows of diamond shapes.

The Crow were stripped naked to the waist. Their entire bodies, including their upper bodies, legs, and faces, were covered with horrible white paint. The way their eyes blinked and peered out from the mask of white paint made them look mysterious, even evil. They wore colorful strings of beads across their chests. Their faces were long. Each man wore long hair woven into two tight braids that fell over each shoulder.

All appearances to the contrary, the Crow were friendly. They were nomadic, having arrived on the Western frontier from Alberta, Canada following the buffalo herds. As a Nation, they had befriended the United States army and supported the Western expansion as scouts. The Crow had fought alongside the 57th Cavalry at the Battle of Little Bighorn and the Battle of Greasy Grass. The Crow were not hostile to the rapid change that came with the discovery of gold and the railroads and the new settlements popping up everywhere. On the contrary, they roamed the prairie following herds of buffaloes

Predictably, the Crow warriors rode up to the stagecoach, spotted me on the buckboard, said nothing, turned their mounts away, and simply vanished. That was it. There was nothing particularly sensational in this encounter. My encounter with the Lakota, on the other hand, scared me halfway to death.

The Lakota showed interest in my stagecoach. They were highly skilled warriors and completely hostile to the Western expansion. They had annihilated Custer's men at the Battle of the Little Bighorn.

I could tell the riders approaching the stagecoach were Lakota. Their bodies were completely covered in baggy buckskin. The buckskin had simple patterns of geometric shapes and abstract shapes of birds. Unlike the Crow, their long hair was unbraided and parted down the middle of their heads. Their hair flowed in the breeze as they bounced on saddles mounted over colorful saddle cloths.

I held my finger snug against the trigger of my .38. The .38 was under my apron. The sight of Lakota triggered heightened breathing. My shotgun was leaning against the buckboard, still untouched.

I didn't want to excite the Lakota. They might have been spoiling for a fight. Their faces were bronze and wide, like Eskimos. They weren't as tall as Crow warriors, and they didn't paint their bronze skin.

Two curious feathers were stuck in headbands at the back of their heads, fully erect. Each rider carried a spear, not a firearm.

The Lakota eased their mounts and rode alongside of the stagecoach. I let the team plod along. There was no point in trying to outrun two Lakota warriors on ponies. It would have been foolhardy to try, so I didn't object to the warriors joining the parade. I waited to act until there was a sign the warriors intended to make a move to stickup the stagecoach.

The Lakota didn't speak. However, their eyes spoke volumes. Their eyes searched me for signs of fear. There were none. Their eyes curiously searched the empty stagecoach. Their eyes squinted at the rifle. Then, they made eye contact with me. This was their way of informing me that they knew I was armed.

The Lakota remained casual on their ponies, walking so slowly alongside the stagecoach that the hooves of the ponies dragged in the dust. After the Lakota satisfied themselves that they had erased any doubt in my mind that they lacked confidence, they fell out of line, stopped their mounts, and simply watched as my team kept after the trail ahead. I looked back over my shoulder. The Lakota were gone.

I snapped the reins at the team. The team complied. We were back on the open trail toward Billings.

This story may not have thrilled the reporter, but every line of it was true. The Indians never bothered me, and I never bothered the Indians. I guess you would say it was a case of mutual respect.

Chapter Twenty-Eight

I stopped looking at the reporter. Instead, I stared at a random spot on the newsroom wall. I looked at that wall like the wall was a spot I tried to detect on a ridge off on Wolf Mountain. The memory of the Civil War years, and thoughts of the Crow and Lakota, swept my mind completely off into a daydream. The reporter gave me time to recover. He didn't rudely interrupt. After a fashionable period of time, he politely broke the daydream.

"Are you okay, Mary?"

"I want to stay on this beautiful land for the rest of my days. In order to change it, to see it progress, it needs to happen out here the same way the rest of the nation evolved. For example, the railroads took over from the stagecoaches. That event made change happen. Without the railroads, Montana would have remained wild, don't you think? The way folks get along has to happen the same way. Something has to improve to help us progress, so we can advance. We aren't allowed to curse in church because it's a church, right?"

"Curse or draw a weapon," the reporter interrupted, emphasizing to me that he had paid careful attention to everything I said. He wanted to alert me that I might be venturing into hypocrisy.

"Curse or draw weapons, yes," I said, ignoring the larger point about hypocrisy. "The same way we can't curse or act a fool in church should apply to the whole nation. I think hate speech or acting a fool should be outlawed everywhere in the nation, like it is banned in church, because the nation is a church, too. I think this ban would do for the nation what the railroad did for the Pacific Northwest. I think it would get done all of the other things Mr. Lincoln had in mind. I think that was what Mr. Lincoln was trying to get across to us."

"Are you planning to ever leave Montana? For instance, do you ever see yourself going back to Ohio or Mississippi?"

"Or Tennessee?" I asked rhetorically, emphasizing that the reporter might possibly not have listened to my story as carefully as he believed.

Did he actually think I would consider going backward in life? If so, why not go all the way back to my origins as a slave in Tennessee?

"What's the news this week? What are you writing about? What's going to be on the front page?" I asked, trying to lighten the mood.

"We are running stories on the Woodrow Wilson administration, Grand Central Station in New York, the world's largest train station, has reopened, and rumors about a filmmaker's plans to secretly film the greatest movie ever made, a movie about the Civil War."

"What's the movie called?"

"Birth of a Nation. It's supposed to be the first ever speakie. Imagine how fast things are changing."

"Seems most things are changing rapidly while other things are staying exactly the same."

"You know how to read, Mary?"

"I learned on the plantation. I was field, but I got chances to get to the house where I was around reading. I paid attention the best I could until I picked it up, secretly of course."

"Do you ever get a little homesick, like think about missing folks back in Tennessee?"

"No, I want to stay on the beauty of this land in Montana for as close to forever as I can get."

The reporter was a very thoughtful fellow. The interview wasn't over. He asked more questions about the adventures of Mary Fields—"Stagecoach" Mary Fields, pioneer. However, I had already reported the crux of what happened. The rest remained open to speculation.

Epilogue

"Stagecoach" Mary Fields, the lion of women's rights, human dignity, really, met her demise, as the legend goes, on an open field in Montana. Suffering from failing health and advanced age, she *elected* to collapse on the prairie, the one place on earth where she knew it was impossible for her to die alone.

In her final hour, she was apparently confident that the indelible bond, the pact, she formed with Montana would not be broken. There really was nothing left, except mountains, sky, and dust. Nothing else. On her dying day, you might say she left history behind her. You might even say she was born again.

This poetic end to her life would have become the stuff of myth, except it didn't exactly end in a poetic way. Instead, a couple of locals happened upon her body on the field while she was still clinging to life. They rushed her to Columbus Hospital in Great Falls. There, Mary Fields was pronounced dead.

The attending physicians listed liver failure as the official cause of death. Today, her grave is modestly marked by a common field stone at Hillside Cemetery in Cascade County. The words, Mary Fields, are written on the stone in unsteady hand.

About the Author

James Ciccone was born in Auburn, New York. He graduated Colgate University with a B.A. in Religion and earned a law degree at Albany Law School of Union University.

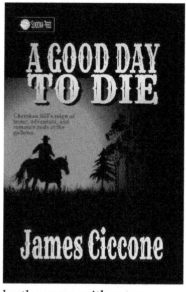

You don't want to make me mad. I've got a lot of hate in me, and I am not afraid of one blessed thing in this life. I'm Crawford Goldsby—better known as Cherokee Bill—and if you think you're the one to bring me to justice you're wrong...dead wrong.

They call me a half-breed, but I killed my first man by the time I was twelve, and I never stopped. Why? Because I like killing—and I'm damn good at it. Indian Territory wouldn't be the same without me.

But this outlaw likes living, too, and when I rob that train carrying millions for a big payoff here in Indian Territory, I've got a plan to cut loose and run to South America—along with my fancy woman, Maggie.

Don't get in my way. Indian Territory is mine. Oklahoma Territory is mine. If you cross me, your life is mine, too. I'm barely eighteen, and I can deliver a kill shot without even looking your way—yes, I'm that good.

Judge Parker can't wait to get his hands on me over in Fort Smith. If he does, death by hanging will be end of me. Will Parker get his wish? We'll see...I've gotten confident in my own abilities to escape. If he gets his way at last, he won't see Cherokee Bill running scared.

I'll look the bastard in the eye and say, "It's **A GOOD DAY TO DIE**..."

Made in the USA
Middletown, DE
10 June 2021